The Screaming Alice
Veronica Thornton

V.J. Thornton

To Mike, Rosa and Joe and in memory of my parents Avis and David who were
always encouraging.

ISBN 978-1-5272-1086-8

Disclaimer
This is a work of fiction inspired by real events. All characters are from the author's
imagination.

Acknowledgements
Lordship Lane Station, 1871, Camille Pissarro, reproduced by permission of The
Samuel Courtauld Trust, The Courtauld Gallery, London
Subway photo © Nick Catford
Railway tickets © Brian Halford

A CIP catalogue record for this book is available from The British Library.

Project management and editing by Cambridge Editorial www.camedit.com
Design by Paul Barrett Book Production www.pbbp.co.uk
Printed and bound in the UK by Short Run Press

'I believe that one place closely explored will yield more than continents passed through.'
Lucy M. Boston from *Stranger at Green Knowe*

'Then the Crystal Palace came, for ever spoiling the view through all its compass, and bringing every show-day from London, a flood of pedestrians down the footpath who left it filthy with cigar ashes for the rest of the week; then the railroads came, and expiating roughs by every excursion train, who knocked the palings about, roared at the cows, and tore down what branches of blossom they could reach...'
John Ruskin *Praeterita*

Prologue

PAMELA

There is just a big barking dog, an Alsatian, tied up outside the caravan. I can't see any puppies. He goes inside to speak to the old man and there are no puppies in there either. I feel bad. I've never bunked off school before. I have a tight feeling in my chest. Is it all for nothing? Are we too late? Has the old man already killed the puppies? I want a cuddly little puppy to look after. I have been looking forward to it so much. I can't help crying and it's difficult to stop. He puts his hand on my shoulder and says he's sorry the puppies are gone. But I still can't stop crying.

He walks away a few steps and says he wants to show me something. It's a special place, a secret and hidden place that no one knows about. It will make up for the puppies. We won't have had a wasted journey.

I'm still shaking a bit and half crying, but also curious. The dog has stopped barking. We have to climb back up the steps, but just before the top there is an opening with a cover that he lifts off. He says we have to go down there, and shows me the ladder. I am still upset and wipe my face on my sleeve. I am a bit unsure but also interested in exploring secret places. It is a bit of a squeeze with my rucksack. He says I should take it off but I won't. At the bottom of the ladder is a tunnel.

June

SALLY

It was a beautiful evening in early summer. Sally enjoyed being on the top deck of the bus by herself, where the evening light cast long, warm shadows across the empty seats and tree branches brushed the open windows as the bus climbed Blackheath Hill. The sun was on her back as she walked directly across the grass, ignoring the many roads and paths that criss-crossed the heath.

The house stood behind a semicircle of grass. It was the end of a row of six, none exactly the same; Sally thought they might be Georgian but wasn't sure. She would have to ask John, her friend from college. She knocked twice with the brass ring held in the lion's mouth and waited. Standing close to the front door she glanced down to the basement kitchen where someone had laid the table, a small posy of cornflowers in the centre, and smiled with anticipation. She was expected.

'Good, you found it then. Come in. You're the first to arrive.'

John held back the door and she stepped into a hallway that was broad and unexpectedly bright. Looking up the ascending curves of stairs she saw a

3

glass dome that spilled the evening light back down to the rug at her feet. Sally smiled appreciatively. An ornate mirror hung above a dark wooden chest. A pack of bacon and a pile of clean sheets were side by side on the chest.

She followed John down a flight of stairs and entered a room that made her gasp. A large semi-basement kitchen was filled with the evening sun from the garden, bathing everything in tones of pink and honey.

It was still, like a stage set with perfect lighting, awaiting actors, and it was quiet. Any noise was softened and muffled by the kitchen being lower than the heath at the front, and the enclosure of the ragged garden glimpsed from the back. Low golden light found its way through windows half covered by leaves and tiny flowers and falling in strong, warm patches onto pale lino.

Sally was entranced. 'What a lovely room.'

The overall impression was one of timelessness. All the objects in that room seemed to fit comfortably together, anchored by two hundred years of comings and goings. In the coming weeks, Sally would try to explain to her friends why she had felt so drawn to the house. She couldn't fully put it into words but she sensed in that kitchen a delicate accumulation of other times, a feeling of preservation and a residue of past concerns and conversations.

In the coming years, Sally would try to explain to herself the powerful pull the house, and in particular the kitchen, had on her. The combination of a hazy history with the exact strong light, smells and warmth of early summer, was a heady mix. She felt she had arrived at somewhere significant.

There were six guests for the unusual meal of spinach soup, potato and Gruyère cheese casserole and fresh strawberries. Syrupy juice trickled down the side of the strawberry bowl onto the white cloth already covered with circles of red wine. No one bothered about stains – at home, a legion of mats would have been enforced. Sally wondered if she could learn to cook such sophisticated but simple meals.

It got so late that Sally was invited to stay. She and Rachel, one of the other guests, were given John's room at the top of the house, the window wide open to the hot summer garden. They chatted drowsily into the night, Sally telling stories about her family and Rachel relating tales of her Russian grandparents. Sally finally fell asleep to the sound of a train passing somewhere nearby. The following morning she awoke to sunshine, and lifted the sash window to look down into the garden. From that height, the smudged geometry of old rose beds was visible, with a central bird bath and thick brick wall like a seam dividing the space of the next garden and a whole row of gardens as far as she could see.

The handsome, slightly down-at-heel house had left a deep impression on her, and as she left, closing the front door behind her, Sally's mind was made up. She was determined to rent a room there and just had to find out how that could be done.

September

WILSON

The girl was still missing.

Several days after her disappearance, the police moved into the school. Detective Inspector Raymond Wilson drove his Rover into the one empty space near the main entrance. Neither he nor his passenger, PC Donald Reid, got out. This was a school they had visited before and they were not in a hurry to go inside.

It was a glorious day and the two men took a few moments to appreciate the morning as the sun shone on their arms through the open car windows. It had been a remarkable summer, one heat wave flowing into another, the hottest summer of the seventies so far. London's lidos had been crowded and given a new unexpected lease of life, as had forgotten English seaside hotels. Why pay for the Costa del Sol when guaranteed sun was on your doorstep?

Part of the policemen's reluctance to go inside arose from the nature of what they had to do. Missing children cases had a gloomy track record of success and so far the lack of any leads whatsoever gave Wilson a bad feeling in the stomach.

Don sat back and lit himself a cigarette.

Wilson leaned across the polished walnut dashboard and opened the glove compartment where, after fumbling and rustling, he found two toffees. As he stuffed the sweet papers into his pocket, he looked up and noticed a boy at the far end of the playground. The kid threw his bag over the fence, then climbed over it himself, picked up the bag and took off towards the local shops.

Wilson frowned. 'Typical,' he muttered to himself.

He felt this school was too big – as most schools seemed to be these days. How were you supposed to keep tabs on so many kids? It had been built on the grounds of an old nursing home and a cluster of rambling villas, all knocked down over twenty years earlier. Various large old trees, ancient survivors of the swathes of forest that used to cover the whole area, were randomly scattered around the edge of the playground and softened the stiff geometry of the rectangular 1950s building. Wilson's idea of what a school should be was entirely based on his own: a local Victorian block of brick that stood near to the Thames and had seemed to absorb some of the river's dampness. Violence had been part of the fabric of the building, from the roughly carved names on the wooden desks to the chipped walls and kicked-in doors. The teachers caned the boys, cuffed them round the back of the head or pushed them up against the wall. The boys punched each other in the playground, egged on by circles of chanting mates. Their fathers, many of whom worked in the docks or the barracks, hit their sons at home. It was the way things were sorted out, quickly and cleanly. It didn't mean anything. There was kindness, too, and as a nipper Wilson (Raymond in those days) would often visit Mrs Green with a black eye or cut knee. As the school secretary, she would comfort anyone and everyone with strong sweet tea, and her office was like an auntie's sitting room with crocheted cushions and a fierce gas fire.

Most importantly, all the teachers knew the names of all the boys.

Both men got out of the car and Wilson put on and buttoned his jacket. He felt uncomfortable in plain clothes and would always prefer to be in uniform. It helped differentiate between his work and home life, something that had become increasingly important to him as he had risen through the ranks.

'Ah, Detective Inspector Wilson. Good morning.'

Miss Lloyd, a smartly dressed woman in her sixties, held the door open for him.

'The headmaster will see you in fifteen minutes; you know where his office is. I hope the old geography room will be suitable for your needs.'

Wilson approved of the room and noted with satisfaction the wide wooden desk with a typewriter and the new red telephone plugged in by the window. He had all he needed. There were a variety of posters on the wall: a cross-section of a coal mine, a diagram of a glacier and a garishly coloured photo of Zurich. On the wall opposite the desk was a stained map of London. He stood back to get a better view. It was large, about 4 ft by 3 ft, and mostly coloured light brown; the Thames was a pale turquoise snake.

Stanford's contoured map of LONDON 1928.

Wilson could study maps like these for hours, translating the flat lines of Dulwich Common into the swoops and dips of Forest Hill where the black lines became increasingly closer and almost touched each other. He thought of his dad helping him to make a papier-mâché landscape for his train set. He was eleven or twelve and they were in the dining room on a winter's afternoon. His dad had shiny black hair and was bending over the dining room table casting giant shadows from the central ceiling light over a range of mountains.

Don pushed noisily through the doorway interrupting his thoughts.

'This is the last box. Give me your keys and I'll lock the car.'

The mother of the missing girl had come to the station that morning as she had done every day for the past week. Wilson understood she wanted the routine of doing something, to get out of the flat, away from the countless reminders, the pyjamas on the bed, the sparkly slippers underneath, the plastic bangle in the bathroom. He had seen these pathetic things on his first visit, the mother smoking cigarette after cigarette, sitting on the edge of the sofa, distracted and numb with worry. Wilson had to write a report and establish facts, and while the mother wanted to help she could hardly speak and her voice shook throughout the interview. There were just the two of them living in the flat, mother and daughter. A smattering of relatives lived nearby: a grandmother in Lewisham, an aunt in Catford and a cousin in the army, the Middle East. No one knew where the father was. He hadn't been seen for over ten years.

So every day the mother walked down to the police station. She didn't phone from her neighbour's flat or from the one phone box that hadn't been vandalised on the corner of the main road; she came to see him. He wished he had something to tell her.

Don was now absorbed by the details on the old map showing familiar yet altered places.

'Hey, Ray, was Thamesmead built on the Plumstead Marshes?'

'Yeah, I think it was.'

'I can't stand that place. I was up there last Tuesday, kids nicking cars left, right and centre. I lose all sense of direction and those roundabouts make me dizzy. It can't be healthy building houses on marshland. I mean, it's just asking for trouble.'

Wilson put his forefinger on the map, where it left a slightly greasy mark.

'This is where the search party will meet on Sunday. It will work outwards all the way to the museum and right the way up to One Tree Hill.

'Do you expect a good turnout?'

'Well, yeah, I hope so. It's been advertised enough locally and they're still showing the Pamela Webb photo on national telly. You can't go anywhere round here without seeing that face peeping out from shop windows, park noticeboards, libraries. Here, have a look at this.' He passed a newspaper to Don who read the headline out loud:

HAVE YOU SEEN THIS GIRL?

Underneath a large photo that took up almost the whole front page of the local newspaper was the now familiar face of Pamela. In it, the girl was a year younger, smiling for the school photographer, a chipped tooth and velvet Alice band pulling the hair back, her eyes dark with a slight hesitancy.

Missing schoolgirl Pamela Webb.

Don continued:

'Pamela Webb, 11 years old, was last seen outside the school gates of Woodlands Comprehensive on Monday 25th September. She was wearing her school uniform underneath a blue anorak with a fur trim hood and carrying a pink rucksack. If anyone saw Pamela on that day, especially after 1pm, please contact the police as a matter of urgency.
This Sunday there will be a search in the parks and wasteland around Pamela's home. All volunteers should meet at 10am by the war memorial.'

Don passed the paper back to Wilson who tore the page out and stabbed it to the board with a drawing pin.

A door slammed outside, a teacher shouted and footsteps receded.

'Come on Don, we need to go and speak to the headmaster.'

The two policemen stepped out into the corridor just as a bell started ringing and they struggled upstream against the tidal wave of children.

SALLY

Two storeys up, and on the other side of the building, Sally heaved a sigh of relief that the lesson was over. The only time the class had been completely quiet was when she had bellowed, 'Right, no one leaves until there is silence. We can stay here all break if you want to.' Apparently, they didn't want to, and a few of them started to sit up straight in an exaggerated way with their arms tightly crossed and their chins thrust forward. They were dismissed one by one and the noisy ones soon cottoned on and also sat still. Gradually the class emptied and Sally was left with the clearing up.

She put the drawings in a drawer and took a dirty cloth from the sink. She never minded clearing up whatever mess there was at the end of a lesson. It was quite soothing, wiping away the grey film of charcoal dust on the tables in curving sweeps. It was a physical activity that separated the noisy, sometimes chaotic, lesson from a return to the world of adults and normal conversation. She needed this bridge between the two parts of her life, this no man's land of rinsing pots and swirling paint down plugholes. In the mindless washing and cleaning she brought herself back from the cardboard cut-out figure she was trying to be – distant, firm and in control of a class, to the person she felt she still was – friendly, uncertain and jokey. The two roles had not yet meshed. Some days it worked and others it didn't.

Sally had been at the school for a few weeks. It was her first teaching post and she felt young and overwhelmed by all that was expected in terms of lesson planning, record keeping, but most of all discipline. Some of her classes were well behaved but not always, and it was the unpredictability that made her quite tense. The fourth-year class that had just left was her most challenging and already a few characters were emerging that made her life difficult. There was Sharon, a hard-faced girl with black hair who had a permanent expression of disdain. She would often arrive ten minutes or so after the lesson had started.

'The bus was late. I got held up.'

It was a statement not an apology.

Two boys as tall as men and more developed than the others enjoyed pushing their weight around.

'Hey Carter, we heard you got a new bike.'

This appeared to be a harmless enquiry but could be the start of Carter losing his new pump or lock as the two boys loitered menacingly in the bike sheds after school.

The first week with this class had been a nightmare. The lesson she had prepared did not occupy them for more than fifteen minutes. By the end of it the whole class had become thoroughly restless, and the dark-haired girl was looking at her with what seemed like contemptuous pity. On the second week Sally had decided she needed to deal with a few of the worst behaved pupils.

'Richard and Karl, could you stay behind at the end of the lesson please.'

'Hey, she fancies you, Ricky boy.'

A fat blond boy leaned across the desk and winked.

'I doubt it. She looks like she needs a real man,' chipped in Tracey.

'What do you know about real men? You wouldn't know one if you tripped over him.'

When the class had gone, the two boys stood reluctantly in the doorway. Sally soon realised it had been a mistake to speak to them both at the same time. As she reasoned with them and finally issued a threat of detention, they leaned against the door frame and looked her up and down with faintly lascivious expressions. The boys gave careless promises to improve their behaviour and Sally dismissed them, but as he turned to go Karl puckered his lips and blew her a noisy kiss. She couldn't control her blushes or hide her embarrassment and the two boys sprinted away down the corridor laughing like maniacs.

There had been minor improvements since that second week but nothing was consistent – a good day was followed by a bad. The pattern of the lessons was like a foxtrot: good, good, bad, bad, good. There wasn't really anyone she could ask for advice. On the first day, the head of department had shown her the art room, handed her the keys, and left her to get on with it. She didn't like to bother him as he was always so busy. A tall man, shouting down the long corridors, doors opening and closing, he would appear or disappear abruptly from a classroom. Was it just a matter of time before her lessons were ordered and she was in control?

Her feelings of tension had been added to by a meeting the head master had called that morning. A first-year girl was missing and the police would be having a base in the school. The teachers were asked to cooperate in any way they could and not talk to the press. The story was already in the national newspapers and on television. Sally had never seen the girl, but her disappearance added to the general sense of unease she felt every time she entered the building.

On the journey home, as the bus meandered through the suburbs of south London, Sally's thoughts turned to the house, now her home, on the edge of Blackheath. After that first visit in early summer she had been desperate to live there.

It had been surprisingly easy.

She had returned to see Reg, the landlord, who said she could have a room at the end of August when two people were leaving. He left her to decide between a room at the top overlooking the heath or a larger one on the floor below. She had left the house that day feeling elated. Walking back across the grass she had passed a Punch and Judy tent set up on the heath. Not many children were watching and the traffic noise was off-putting and distracting. Sally thought the puppet man looked old and tired. His job had changed and maybe he was there by habit. He would probably not return the following year. She had stood and watched for a while. His presence seemed related to the house; both were faded and jaded but both represented a strong thread of connection with the past. The travelling performer with his stripy tent and threadbare puppets confirmed her opinion that she was moving into a place of colour and history.

Sally was jolted back into the present by a sharp, though unintentional knock from a satchel, as a schoolgirl pushed past in a hurry to catch up with her friends. Sally also stood up as they had finally reached her stop.

ALAN

'How much am I bid for these beautiful vases? Lot 324, Royal Doulton, start me at £10, anyone at £10? Yes, you sir, and you madam, am I bid £12? Yes madam, any advance on £12? Gentleman in the corner, do I hear £15? Yes, we have £15. Any advance on £15? Two Royal Doulton vases going for £15, that is your final offer Sir? So, selling at £15, going, going, gone. Sold to the gentleman in the corner. Thank you very much, ladies and gentlemen. Now, Lot 325, a rosewood music cabinet. Who will start the bidding?'

Alan stood in the corner of the auction room quite close to the door. He wasn't really interested in the items on sale today. It was mainly furniture and bits of china, and his area was maps and prints, but he always attended all the auctions and enjoyed the atmosphere of what he had now come to consider his work.

'Lot 326, a Spode dog bowl.'

A man in a green tweed jacket caught Alan's eye and grinned. Fifteen minutes later they were both standing at the counter of the tea bar.

'Two teas, please, Betty, and a couple of those buns. Yes, the ones with sugar on top, Bath buns, is that what you call them?'

Betty lifted the huge teapot with effort and then transferred the sticky buns from under a plastic dome to a blue stripy plate. All the crockery on the counter was a colourful collection of rejects from various sales. Spotted 1950s plates were stacked with faded willow pattern and the occasional Wedgewood. Alan stirred sugar into a thick white cup and rested the spoon on a rose-patterned saucer.

He started telling Rob about the newly acquired room that he was sub-letting at the back of the antique shop.

'It's not exactly spacious, but anything will be better than another winter freezing outside on the market. You'll have to come and see it. Anyway, how are you? Bought anything today?'

Rob brushed some sugar from his tartan tie and took a swig of his tea before replying.

'Not bad, not bad at all, and yes, I've just acquired an interesting box of books. Very useful, very useful indeed.'

'What do you mean "useful"? Will they fetch a good price?'

'Well, in a roundabout sort of way.'

Rob glanced around the tea bar, which was beginning to empty now. Betty was piling cups and plates onto a trolley and throwing cutlery into a steaming bowl of soapy water. She had an all-purpose cloth tucked into the belt of her apron that she used to wipe the Formica table tops, the seats of chairs and the three mirrors that ran along the wall. Outside on the staircase, various boxes were being lifted or bumped down to waiting vans below. Betty disappeared behind a faded chintz curtain to a back kitchen and started washing up.

'Have you got a spare half hour? You could come to my shop and I'll show you what I'm doing with the books.' Rob stubbed his cigarette out on a saucer.

Out in the street, the two men turned towards the river and walked briskly until they reached the expanse of concrete that surrounded the old tea clipper, the Cutty Sark. They stopped and leaned on the wall by the steps that went down into the chalky brown water, a randomly preserved fragment of the old river frontage.

Rob turned his back to the wind and tried to light a cigarette under his jacket. From here you could just make out the old frontage of the Deptford Dockyard beyond the upturned table of Deptford Power station. Both men knew it wasn't necessary to take this roundabout route to Rob's shop but they needed little excuse to check on the river traffic or the direction of the tide. Alan in particular liked coming here to remind himself where he was in the world. Close to this river, on zero degrees longitude, seemed a very good personal map reference. Rob's shop was in a side street that led to the park. It was narrow but well lit near the front, progressing into stages of dinginess the further back you went. A young woman sat at a desk near the window, bent over a book, with a scalpel in her hand.

'Hallo Alison. How's it going?'

'Not bad. I sold three books and five postcards this morning.' She opened a red book and showed Rob a new foolscap sheet with carefully ruled columns containing titles and amounts of money neatly written in blue black ink.

'What are you doing, Alison? Cutting up books?' Alan perched on the edge of the desk.

'You see, Alan, this is what I wanted to talk about. Take a chair.' Rob carefully lifted a pile of frames onto the floor.

'Sit here. Now, the books I bought this morning are engravings of London, mainly mid-nineteenth century. There are three volumes, south, south-west, and best of all, south-east London. Loads of images of this area, which is just what the tourists want as souvenirs. A reminder of a place they have visited, still recognisable, but a hundred years or so earlier.'

'So this is where I come in.' Alison stood up and reached for a box on a shelf.

'I cut out the engravings from the book, then we get students from the local art college to give them a wash of colour and we frame them, like this.'

She held up two small wooden frames; one showed the Greenwich Observatory in autumn, the other a windmill on Blackheath.

'By the way, Rob, one of the students was here earlier. He brought back this box and took another. I paid him what we agreed, is that OK?'

'Who was it? Are they any good?'

'Yes, they're fine. It was that Turkish fellow, I can't remember his name but he has beautiful brown eyes. He asked me to have coffee with him. Alison looked at Rob in a mildly challenging way.

'Let's see. As long as it wasn't that Geordie bloke. He was too slapdash for words, so don't give him any more for God's sake.' He flicked through the box.

'Yes, these are good, all up to standard. Did you have coffee with him?'

Alan was weary of the games these two played.

'What's this got to do with me? You asked me here to discuss something.'

'Ah, yes, well, I just thought there should be a little distance between selling books and selling prints cut out of books. So I thought you might be able to shift a few these of these prints in your new place. You can see how they go and take a percentage for yourself naturally.'

'I don't know, Rob. It does seem a bit destructive, a sort of vandalism.'

'More people get to see the prints though. They're not hidden away on a rich person's bookshelf. Think of it as a kind of redistribution of wealth in the form of images.'

Alan smiled at this crude attempt to appeal to what Rob thought were his politics.

'Yeah, OK, why not? I'll give it a go. You'll deal with the art students and the framing though?'

'Yes, of course,' said Alison swiftly, with an oversweet, creamy smile.

'Good man. You won't regret this. There's money to be made believe me. Oh, by the way, I've got a book for you.'

Rob disappeared into the gloom at the back of the shop and Alison turned to put the prints back on the shelf.

'I got it a couple of months back and have been meaning to give it to you ever since. It's about that old railway you're interested in. You know, Greenwich to Crystal Palace. That's the one, isn't it?

'Thank you. I'll enjoy this.'

Alan smiled and carefully flicked through a few pages.

He fitted the book into his jacket pocket, said goodbye to both his friends, then stepped out into the street.

As he walked towards the park he thought of the first time, about ten years ago, that he had met Rob, red haired, and sitting in the college refectory, absent-mindedly stirring a cup of tea and reading Proust in a studiously casual sort of way.

They had sat next to Alison at the first lecture on their history of art course. In the first year, their friendship was a useful triangle. They complemented each other and their personalities formed a good balance. By the end of the first summer it became obvious that Rob and Alison were considering a deeper relationship, despite Rob's consistent pursuit of 'skirt'. Alan started to feel like a piggy in the middle but just as he was tiring of this role he met Fiona and his life changed completely.

He had reached the top of the hill and stopped as always to look back at the river. Groups of tourists were taking photos by the statue of General Wolfe, and Alan sat near them. He could see roughly where he and Rob had stood earlier, the masts of the Cutty Sark guiding his vision. He looked left towards St Paul's then to Deptford, the Isle of Dogs, and the Naval College straight ahead. Sweeping round to the right he could see the power station and widening river leading to Woolwich and beyond to Gravesend. He had collected many prints of this view, and different images from history superimposed themselves in his head: the scratchy masts of tall ships, the brown-red sails of the Thames barges, the dirty smoke from the tugs and left-over cranes from the docks. In his mind, the river was chock-a-block; in reality it was clear, calm and more or less empty. Alan felt the book in his pocket that Rob had given him earlier as he stood up and walked towards the heath and his home.

PAMELA

I was playing with Caroline on the steps at the bottom near the rubbish chute. We were just messing about with a ball and scooter. Sometimes it's boring in the summer holidays. We've finished junior school for ever and are looking forward to big school. This morning me and Caroline went to the shops to buy a bra. We've planned it for weeks while we saved up the money. Only one of our friends had a bra in the junior school, Janet Prendergast. We saw her in P.E. It looked nice, like two brown eggs in white egg-cups. So me and Caroline wanted one. We decided to share it as we didn't have enough money for one each. I needed one more than Caroline because it feels wobbly when I play netball and I am goal attack.

We went to Woolworths because you can look and take them out the packet. We felt them and decided that 32A might be a good size. We couldn't decide on turquoise, lemon or white but finally chose white because it would match most of our knickers.

It was so exciting coming out of Woolworths with our small crunchy bag. We stopped in the park on the way home and Caroline tried it on in the toilets. When we got back to the flats I went into my bedroom and put it on. I kept it on when we were playing by the rubbish chute. My chest felt a bit bigger and harder and I felt all grown up. Caroline kept accidently on purpose brushing up against me whispering 'itsy bitsy titsy' and we were both laughing.

This big girl with black hair came over to us. I'd seen her around before. I think she lives in the next block but I've never spoken to her. She is older and looks hard and I'm a bit frightened of her. As she walked towards us I noticed her tits were quite big in her tight white t-shirt. She had stubble under her arms and her forehead was a bit sweaty. We were both surprised when she spoke to us.

'Hey, you two, do you want to earn some money?'

SALLY

Reaching the wide expanse of heath, Sally turned towards the house and stood close to the front door, fumbling for her key. As usual she looked down to the basement kitchen to see if anyone was there, but only the cat was curled up on the chair asleep. Stepping into the hallway, she looked up as she heard footsteps.

'Sally, is that you?'

John jumped the last three steps and landed in front of her on the plum red carpet.

'I'm looking for a bottle opener. We're having drinks on the roof. Come and join us.'

She followed John down the stairs to the kitchen.

'On the roof?'

'Yes, you probably didn't realise it was there. You have to go through the bathroom.'

Sally was puzzled. She didn't know what John meant. She put her bags on the nearest chair and reached for the kettle, filling it from the cracked butler sink and lighting the gas.

'How do you get onto the roof from the bathroom?'

'Ah ha, this house is full of surprises. Anyway, come up when you're ready. You'll see the trapdoor in the ceiling – oh, and bring an extra glass.'

John took the bottle opener and Sally heard him bounding back up the stairs. She needed to sit quietly for a moment, make some tea and calm herself from the frenzied day. She sat at the table waiting for the kettle to boil. There had been a horrible incident in her fourth-year lesson that morning. Needing more space to mix paints, Sally had moved the guillotine, used for cutting paper, away from the wall and onto the old black printing press that stood by the door. Near the end of the lesson Karl had been leaning against the press, waiting for the bell, and keen to leave. Sally had asked everyone to sit down but as usual Karl and Richard were doing their own thing. A scream of pain was followed by the door being flung open and Karl rushing out closely followed by Richard. Sally turned from the sink; the bell hadn't rung yet. 'What's going on? Where's Karl gone?'

'He's cut his finger off,' a boy called Nick informed her calmly.

'Oh, don't be so stupid.'

The door was flung open again and Les, the art technician, came in looking for Karl's finger. In fact, it was just the tip. There was a small piece of flesh on the floor under the guillotine that Les scooped up.

'He didn't do it on purpose Miss.'

The class were shocked into silence as Nick explained what had happened. Karl had had his hand resting on the guillotine and was looking the other way as Richard had thoughtlessly pulled the handle down.

'He didn't mean to do it.' Nick was adamant.

The bell rang for the end of lesson but no one moved. Sally felt very shaky. Sharon, the hard-faced girl with black hair, came to stand next to Nick.

'Don't worry Miss, it was just an accident.'

She did worry though and couldn't get the incident out of her mind. On the bus home, she kept seeing that grisly little piece of flesh on the floor. If only she hadn't moved the guillotine. If only Karl and Richard had been sitting down like everyone else. Apparently, Les had taken Karl to hospital where the end of his finger had been sewn back on. She was relieved at this information but still quite shaken at what could happen so quickly when your back was turned.

Sally poured boiling water into the teapot, took a cup from the draining board and returned to the table, glad to be left alone in the peaceful old kitchen. She sat opposite the fireplace looking at a row of old meat platters arranged high on the mantle shelf. They were an assortment of blue and white patterns with mottled brown veins. She knew this was a process that happened to old china but it made her think both of long ago gravy and miniature maps.

A boiler had been wedged into the chimney breast, by the look of it some time in the 1950s. Two red and cream gas cookers from the same era, shiny with grease, stood next to a double butler sink under the window. A plastic topped table where Sally sat drinking her tea filled the middle of the work area nearest to the garden and back door. Another table stood just a few feet away and provided the transition to the dining area. A couple of faded linen chairs, one with a sleeping cat, and an upright piano, confirmed this impression.

Sally heard a shriek of laughter and a thud outside on the stairs. John returned with two of his friends, Pete and Nancy, both carrying wine glasses.

'Hallo Sally. Good God this house is creepy. I don't recommend the loo in the coal hole out there. There must be spiders. Petey come with me. I want to show you.'

Nancy yanked Pete's hand, her many bangles jangling noisily, and wrenched him out of the room. John held a wine bottle between his knees and proceeded to open it, painfully slowly. Sally could hear the faint squeak of the cork. He then poured the warm wine into four different sized glasses and disappeared momentarily, returning with a tray of ice.

'Those two can't keep their hands off each other.'

He put one piece of ice into each glass then opened the door slightly and shouted.

'Come on you two, have another drink.'

John opened a packet of crisps and tipped them into a yellow plastic bowl.

'Are you coming, Sally? The view is pretty good up there.'

They all climbed the three flights of stairs to the top of the house, John holding a bottle of wine and Nancy slopping her drink as she carried it precariously, and squeezed into the bathroom. It felt strange to have such a crowd of people in a normally private space. Sally noticed another thin view of the garden through the half-open window and began to think of ideas for possible paintings. Ideas were all she had time for since leaving college in the summer. The teaching had expanded to fill every corner of her brain.

Pete went first up the rickety step ladder. It didn't look very safe to Sally. Many things didn't look very safe after today's horrible incident. Nancy followed, spilling her wine but refusing to let anyone else hold her glass. John pushed her gently from behind and looked back at Sally.

'OK?'

She nodded and followed carefully up the wobbly ladder. Squeezing through the small square space, she found herself surrounded by chimneys and roof tiles. Nancy was reclining on an old sleeping bag and some Turkish cushions, while Pete stood looking across the heath through binoculars. John took Sally's hand and moved her to the edge.

'Look.'

She smiled as a whole new vista came into view. The extra height simplified the geometric shapes of the lower buildings, defined the green curve of grass in front of them and gave glimpses of otherwise hidden spaces. To the south, an invisible railway was hidden by trees; to the west, the roof continued across to the next three or four houses; to the east, beyond other gardens, was the village, and cars passed by noiselessly on the heath.

September

Sally took off her shoes and warmed her bare feet on the lead of the roof.

'We seem to be above the level of noise here. I can't hear the traffic at all.'

John handed Sally a glass of wine and Nancy held up her empty one.

'Come and sit down here, Sally.' She patted a cushion and held her empty glass higher, where it caught the pink of the sinking sun.

Sally sank back into the soft cushion, splayed her toes and breathed deeply. She was starting to feel a bit more relaxed. She closed her eyes and once again saw the tip of finger on the floor. She breathed deeply. A train passed by at the bottom of the garden. As it receded, so, gradually, did her thoughts of her difficult day. She could begin to forget the guillotine incident, but she must be more careful in future. She wouldn't think about the fighting in the corridors, the pushing and shouting and the chaos of her lessons. She didn't need to plan anything or check her timetable or worry about the missing girl; it could all wait until tomorrow. Now, on this beautiful evening in late summer, she could just enjoy being cocooned up here on the roof with her friends.

WILSON

DI Ray Wilson stood frowning as he stared at his list. This search party for Pamela Webb had deprived him of his Sunday cooked breakfast. Crispy bacon, soft eggs and bronzed mushrooms had given way to half a cup of tea and a biscuit. Not a good start to the day.

The first three groups had set off. The two remaining groups waiting for instructions were a mixed crew of pupils from the school, parents, pensioners, grandparents, kids in pushchairs, neighbours and shopkeepers – anyone and everyone from the local area. Some had even brought their dogs. As they set off in a straggly line, beating the grass with their sticks, their mood seemed almost festive. Coming together as a community gave them a chance to gossip, catch up with friends, chat with neighbours, so that momentarily they forgot the darker purpose of their gathering.

As the last two groups set off, Wilson turned to his journalist friend.

'Make sure you get a shot of the coloured kid, the one in the soldier's uniform. I'm nipping up to the café in the museum to get a bacon sandwich.'

When he returned, two old men from the first search party were sitting on camping stools. They waved their sticks in greeting to Wilson and seemed keen to talk.

'We were just reminiscing about the Crystal Palace.'

'I still miss it. Such a tragedy when it burned down.'

One of the old men wearing a trilby started to tell a story he had obviously told before. Wilson only half listened, wondering if all this searching would be a waste of time; it usually was. Apparently, the man's cousin had been a policeman and happened to be on the top deck of a bus when he saw flames coming from the Palace. He had stopped the bus immediately and called the fire brigade from the phone box on the parade. The cousin had used his truncheon to smash windscreens so the bus crew could steer the nearby cars to safety.

'They had all the fire engines from right across London turning up. The blaze could be seen from the Channel so they say.'

The man with the trilby turned to Wilson and asked if he had seen the fire. Wilson said that he hadn't, but his father had brought him afterwards to see the ruins. He had been impressed by the sheer size and scale of it.

The man nodded in agreement.

'Yes, it's left such a gap.'

Wilson stood and talked to them for a while, mulling over the different bits of land that needed to be searched: the old railway lines, the allotments, scraps of wasteland. On the hill near the museum they had a good vantage point of all these areas. The curve of the current railway lines led the eye across and round and on into the distance. For those that knew where to look, evidence of the old Crystal Palace line, the rails torn up years before, was visible in parts and then vanished under a housing estate only to re-emerge later as a nature walk. There were tunnels left by the railway that would need thorough searching.

The groups of allotments looked peaceful on this Sunday morning, their ramshackle buildings and neat rows of vegetables giving a reassuring sense of order. Curves of thin smoke from bonfires added to the calmness of the 'day of rest', shops were closed and the roads were quiet. Children were bored but free to mess about doing nothing. One of the old men pointed out his particular allotment and talk turned to growing potatoes and carrots. Wilson hoped he wouldn't be having cabbage with his roast dinner.

'Something's happened, look,' said one of the old men.

Two women were running up the hill, gesticulating and shouting.

'We've found some clothes in freshly dug earth just beyond those bushes down there.'

They turned and retraced their steps with Wilson following as fast as the recently digested bacon roll would allow. A beefy man was digging with fierce intent around a hollow piece of dried earth, the sweat pouring from his forehead.

He stood up and leaned on his shovel, his face a dangerous shade of red. The clothing turned out to be a man's thin raincoat and a pair of socks. One of the women bent down to pick them up and Wilson jumped in quickly to stop her.

'Best leave them there, Madam.'

He waved to a couple of police officers standing at the top of the hill and signalled for them to bring some bags.

'Probably left by a tramp sleeping rough.'

This single incident was the only excitement of the day and by one o'clock most of the people had gone home.

Two days later, Wilson pinned a second newspaper article to the board in the old geography room.

This time the headline read:

THE AGONY OF PAMELA'S MOTHER

A distraught Brenda Webb choked back the tears as she told of the nightmare disappearance of her 11-year-old daughter. For 21 days Mrs Webb has lived in agony not knowing if her daughter is alive or dead.

'It's every parent's worst nightmare,' sobbed the mum of Pamela Webb as she told of her anguish since her daughter's disappearance from the school gates three weeks ago.

A massive search on Sunday failed to find any trace of the slim, cheerful girl. Hundreds of police and volunteers joined the search in parks and waste ground around Pamela's home on the Ellis Estate.

The failure of Sunday's hunt has been a bitter blow

*to the family but with the police searching Pamela's
school again and carrying out a house-to-house
search in the area there is still hope.*

*The man leading the hunt, Detective Inspector Ray
Wilson, said: 'Now we are making a concentrated
effort on railway lines in the area.'*

*Police are working on a number of theories, including
the possibility that Pamela has been abducted, but
as yet they have no clues to go on. Every lead, every
possible sighting, is being followed up.*

*But still Pamela's mother Brenda Webb gazes out of
the window of her third-floor flat, stares at Pamela's
photo and anxiously awaits the knock on the door
that could bring total happiness or total heartbreak.'*

The article had been written by Wilson's journalist
friend who was a reporter on the local paper. It had been
Wilson's suggestion that they include another article
written from the point of view of one of the helpers
on the search party. It read as if the lad had written
it himself, even though he hadn't. Wilson's friend had
drafted it then shown it to the young man who just said
'OK'. They took his photo, slipped him a fiver, and that
was it.

There was a sharp knock on the door and Don put
his head into the room.

'Just passing. Have you seen the latest in the local
rag?'

'Yup, already got it here.' He tapped the noticeboard. 'There's another one in *The Press* with a photo. Take a look.'

Wilson passed him the newspaper then returned to sorting a batch of papers from a file. Don sat on the edge of the desk and read from the paper, mouthing the words silently to himself, an old junior school habit.

The headline read: *'I JOIN SEARCH FOR MISSING GIRL'.*

Steven Morley, a young soldier and ex-pupil of Woodlands Comprehensive, took part in the search for Pamela Webb on Sunday.

> 'I was one in a line of over 50 people. We were carrying sticks and we covered swathes of parkland and allotments, beating the undergrowth and bushes. We were half hopeful of finding a clue and half afraid in case we did. We were there for one purpose, to find a trace of the missing girl. There were several false alarms including when someone uncovered some clothes in a mound of freshly dug earth. This brought police and searchers running from every direction, but nothing was found. I've got mixed feelings. I'm sad that all our efforts came to nothing but somehow hopeful that Pamela might still be alive.'

Don screwed up his face.

'Did that soldier really write this?'

'No, it was my mate. You know, Derek the journalist. It's not bad is it?'

The article had a freshness and authenticity. The photo, however, was what pleased him the most. It showed a young coloured man in army uniform and the caption underneath read:

'Steven Morley, currently serving in Northern Ireland, home on leave, joins in the search for Pamela Webb.'

Don grunted.

'So I guess the old man will be pleased. What was it he said?'

Don spoke in a slow deliberate way as if addressing a class of simple children. '"Every opportunity should be taken to show the coloured community in a positive light." So this fits the bill, a soldier, and serving in Northern Ireland. You'll be in his good books no doubt. It all seems a bit phoney to me, I mean the news is the news, no use trying to twist it.'

'Well, that soldier was there. He used to go to this school and he was part of the search party so there's no twisting going on. It's just a matter of selection when it comes to the photo.'

'Yeah, but you know what I mean. They didn't choose a picture of any of the retired coppers or the housewives in the search party, and there were plenty more of them than coloured soldiers.'

'But whatever you think, this is still a strong picture. It makes you want to read the article, doesn't it?'

"Spose so. Anyway I'm off, so I'll see you tomorrow.'

Don threw the paper onto the table and slammed the door.

Wilson wanted a bit of time to think and make sure he had gone through all the files thoroughly in preparation for the interviews tomorrow. He enjoyed the calm of the school after everyone had gone home, with the occasional cleaner sweeping the endless shiny floors of the corridors. Wilson lit another cigarette. He thought the article was good. Derek had done them proud and the photo was the icing on the cake. He did sort of agree with Don though – you didn't need to go looking for a certain type of news. It could get a bit, what was the word? Contrived, yes that was it. He thought of his Uncle Brian who had owned a pub in Brixton in the 1950s, a retired footballer. He would add a few pence to the price of a pint if a coloured man came to the bar. Word would get around and they would choose to drink elsewhere. That seemed to be the way to do it, quietly and politely. No fuss. He didn't object to immigrants in principle; some of them were pleasant enough, but they shouldn't be allowed to take over an area. That's when the trouble started, and that's when English people started moving out and more coloureds moved in and then the balance got unhealthy. Take this school. They were about half and half, exemplified at either extreme by skinheads and Afros. All right for the moment, but he foresaw trouble.

Wilson put the files into the cabinet and locked it. He thought of the missing girl's mother, Brenda, but he still had nothing to tell her. They had hardly anything to go on. As he unlocked his car in the empty car park he remembered it was Tuesday, which meant shepherd's pie. He slung his briefcase in the back and braced himself for the South Circular.

STANLEY

There was a kid hanging around this morning. He was watching from the top of the parade and kept looking down here. He was still there when I came out the caravan. I didn't really take much notice. I don't want to encourage anyone. The next thing I saw he was on the steps. He spent a while fiddling around and seemed to do a bit of digging. What's he up to?

Then he came down, bold as brass, and asked if he could stroke Bessie. She seemed to take to him. I didn't mind too much. We spoke a bit, he said he wants a dog but he's not allowed to have one. He carried on stroking Bessie and asked if he could come and see her again, maybe bring her a bone. Well, I don't see why not. It's up to him.

ALAN

Rob was late as usual. Alan sat at the bar with two pints and resigned himself to a long wait. He sipped his beer and took the slim blue volume *Railway World 1960* from his pocket. Rob had put a postcard to mark the relevant chapter. It was of a Pissarro painting and showed a suburban street seen from across a field.

'Isn't he a bit dull?' had been Rob's comment when Alan had chosen to write his dissertation on Pissarro's paintings in London. Rob's choice had been Francis Bacon, whose sensational life interested him just as much as the paintings. But Alan had lived in the area Pissarro depicted. He had been at school there and was familiar with some of the streets, could identify a curve in the road or the church spire half hidden by smaller trees. Alan was soothed by the views of an emerging suburbia in the 1870s. He appreciated the soft brushstrokes, the glimpses of sky, the comfortable villas and the sense of calm he saw in the paintings. He was presented with a more positive version of the area he had been sent to school in. That had been an unhappy period and the paintings went some way to overlaying those troubled memories. Alan knew the locations of some of the paintings, but not all. He was particularly interested in a painting of a train and its uncertain title *Probably Penge Station*. This uncertainty had caught his interest while a student and contributed to his research on the old railway line. He was pretty sure it wasn't Penge Station but, if not, then where was it?

Alan looked at his watch. Rob was probably with some woman. Despite Alison, he always seemed to have something going on, some new conquest on the horizon, often more than one. His search for women was as much of a routine as cleaning his teeth. A smile, a touch on the arm, anything could happen and often did. The scent of possibility was dabbed on like aftershave for Rob. The thrill of the chase was often more exciting than the kill.

Alan's own experiences were severely limited by comparison. The first had been long ago in the South of France. His father had suggested a family holiday, a reunion of sorts, after five years of his parents living apart. Surprisingly, his mother had agreed, probably as she had thought Alan might appreciate this attempt at being a normal family. Apart from a long weekend in Florence, as part of his degree course, that holiday in Nice had been his only experience of 'abroad'.

So they had filled the boot of the Humber with ridiculous things like toilet paper and tins of corned beef. He had enjoyed everything about that fortnight, driving down poplar-lined roads, stuck behind strangely tall vans with chevrons on the front, eating unusual foods, sterilised milk, even the dark and smelly café toilets were part of the adventure that was not England. The heat made him feel relaxed; there was a sense of liberation and a freedom from clothes. His parents seemed to flourish. His mother in particular looked good in her white shirt and shorts. They both played a lot of tennis and drank small glasses of unusual coloured drinks at dusk. Alan amused himself for most of the day and was only required to turn up for meals at the newly built boxy hotel. He hung around on the beach with some French children, Claude, Pierre and Monique. It was the first time he could remember being interested in a girl or even having access to one. The two boys were about his age, eleven and twelve, but Monique was thirteen and a half, and keen to emphasise her advanced years. She was the first girl Alan had met who wore a bikini, and her small breasts reminded him of fondant fancies. He couldn't take his eyes off them, as if by close observation he might catch them growing. He wasn't interested in the Brigitte Bardot lookalikes, although his father obviously was. They were wobbly, and with their suffocating amounts of flesh there was just too much of them. But Monique was small and hard with sharp elbows and an intense frowning face that both attracted and frightened him. Once, while they were hiding behind a boat, she suddenly turned his face towards her own and kissed him fiercely on the mouth. It was quite painful and fortunately only lasted a few seconds. Then she jumped up and ran away, spraying him with sand. He remembered this tiny but significant incident as there was a yawning gap of almost ten years before a girl or woman showed any interest in him again.

He felt a hand on his shoulder.

'Glad to see you've got the drinks in.'

Rob smiled as he stubbed out his cigarette and picked up a full glass.

'Cheers. Sorry I'm a bit late. Got held up. Had to see someone.'

Alan sighed and took a small sip of beer.

'You must be mad. I mean how much more complicated can you make your life? I take it Alison doesn't know?'

'Obviously, I haven't spelled it out to her. I think she knows something's up but we don't live in each other's pockets. I'm pretty sure she's been flirting with some of the blokes from the art school.'

'There's a big difference between flirting and screwing.'

'Yeah, isn't there just.'

Rob drained his glass and wiped his lips with what Alan felt was too much like lascivious relish.

'Christ, now I understand why you've been wearing that bloody awful tartan tie for the past month.'

'Yup, all part of the plan. It's like subliminal advertising. Give them a little visual sign, make them feel a slight connection. It seems to work more times than not.'

'So that explains the cricket trousers last summer. Let me guess. Was that one Australian? South African?'

'Janet from Sydney, a lifetime of sun on her perfect thighs. My God, she was athletic and so strong.'

'Spare me the details. Do you want another?'

The pub in Blackheath was very smoky and getting more crowded. It was just after midday and the difference between the streets outside, windy and fresh, contrasted greatly with the dim, fusty interior. Various plates of unappetising sandwiches were being passed from a hatch behind the bar and came to rest on a soggy beer mat in front of Alan. A raffle ticket was tucked under a piece of lettuce and the landlady shouted the numbers loudly close to his ears.

'Twenty-three, ham and mustard, twenty-four, cheese and pickle.'

The swirls of smoke seemed to curl the crusts of the bread before a burly man came to claim them and whisked the sandwiches away. The appetite Alan had been building was rapidly diminishing.

'Rob, shall we move on? To be honest I could do with some fresh air.'

Outside, the light hurt their eyes. Alan reached in his pocket for sunglasses and they turned to walk to the heath.

'So, let's get this straight, Rob. You've been knocking off this Scottish nurse. Now she's getting too keen and you're wondering how to get rid of her?'

'Yes, that's it in a nutshell I suppose. I never led her to believe it was anything serious, just some fun.'

'So there's a whole nurse's home full of potential conquests, or victims more like, right on your doorstep. They turn up in your shop, homesick, looking for a card to send to their mum. You're ever so helpful, kind and friendly; "Where are you from? How long have you been here? I could show you some of the sights, the view from the top of the park is one of the best in London. Are you free later? We could go at sunset. Oh, by the way I might push you into a bush and shag you senseless if it seems you won't put up too much of a fight."'

'It's not like that. I don't force myself onto anyone. They're lonely and I offer friendship. If they're keen for more, well why not?'

'Oh, yes, and pay for the cards at the till. That redhead will take the money. She's my girlfriend by the way.'

'I wouldn't do anything in front of Alison. I'm not completely heartless.'

'No, just completely deceitful. Christ, I don't know how you have the nerve or the energy, and it's all so close. The nurse's home is right next door. Surely you must have been seen?'

'I'm not that stupid. Arrangements have to be made. The plotting and the intrigue is all part of the enjoyment. I make it my business to know the local area as thoroughly as possible. Talking of which, have you read that book I gave you about the old railway?'

They had reached a pub on the edge of the heath that stood on the corner of a curve of houses and overlooked a pond fringed by trees. Rob went to get the drinks and despite the wind Alan sat on a bench enjoying the fresh air. He considered Rob and his many sexual exploits. They contrasted greatly with his own limited encounters. Even his father had seemed more successful in that area, which surely wasn't meant to be the case?

One summer, about ten years ago, while he had been a student and visiting his dad in the holidays, Alan had come across Doreen whisking eggs in the kitchen and singing along to a transistor radio. The previous housekeeper had retired and here was a plump sandy haired replacement with an apron pulled tightly across her breasts. Appointed to clean the house, deal with the laundry and cook evening meals, Doreen's main forte was making cakes, which she did with gusto and relish.

As she transferred slices of a moist Victoria sponge from one plate to another, she would stick her tongue out slightly. Alan watched her upper arms, the creamy skin and freckles like the dusted icing sugar on the cake. He noticed a birthmark on her knee as she crossed her legs in her new lemon mini dress and smiled across to Alan's father. She was soft and spongy like her cakes and she smelled good. Alan realised his father was sleeping with her and observed that sex had seemed to break down his snobbery. Suddenly he and Doreen were popping off to the pictures, eating in the Golden Egg and going to the races in Brighton. The house was not very clean, the laundry in piles, but there was always a fresh batch of scones or coffee creams in the kitchen. It was all the wrong way round. There he had been, a young man in the middle of the so-called Swinging Sixties, with no prospect of sex or even a girlfriend, and there was his square middle-aged old dad getting his end away.

Of course, it didn't last. Once Doreen realised marriage was not on the cards, she left and took a job at the local supermarket. But Alan's dad was more relaxed in many ways. He didn't bother with housekeepers after that, all of which left Alan feeling inadequate, lacking in confidence, and frustrated. It may have explained his enthusiasm for Fiona, whom he met a few weeks later. He was grateful she approached him. He appreciated having a ready-made girlfriend and this was more important at the time than who the girlfriend actually was.

'Grab these.' Rob had returned with drinks and a couple of sausage rolls. Alan took the book from his pocket and opened a map, which he spread on the pub table using two beer glasses on opposite corners to hold it flat. As Rob read extracts from the book, Alan traced with a pencil on the map the route the train would have taken from Greenwich to Crystal Palace. It was not the best surface to work on but it didn't take long for the route to emerge.

Alan sat up and finished his drink.

'Well, that's it, more or less. You know, I think I should visit the sites of all the old stations and see what's left, if anything, and try to solve the "Probably Penge" mystery.'

'You mean that old Pissarro painting? Well, I could come with you if you liked. Two heads would be better

48

than one. We could start next Sunday. It could be a weekly or fortnightly visit, each time doing a different station on the route, taking photos, scouting around a bit, visiting a hostelry or two. What do you think?'

Alan hadn't thought of involving anyone else in his project, but now that Rob was offering, it seemed to make sense. He would have someone to discuss things with, to formalise the research and give it structure.

'Could you get hold of a bike?'

'Yeah, I'll borrow Alison's. She won't mind.'

SALLY

'It's criminal, painting over such beautiful wood. What do they want to go and do that for?'

Sally and Mr Booth the geography teacher stood at the top of C staircase. They were on break duty and were positioned to stop children from gaining access to the upper floor. A partition of a wooden frame filled with glass panels fenced off the stairwell.

'What was wrong with a bit of natural wood and varnish? I mean painting it white doesn't look right. It will be scuffed and marked in no time. Utterly impractical.'

Sally wasn't sure what to say. She had no opinions on wood but she liked Mr Booth's accent and his rich throaty voice.

'Where are you from? I can't place your accent. I think it's northern isn't it?'

'Newcastle.'

He said the first part of the word without moving his lips but on 'castle' the left side of his mouth opened to expose teeth and travelled up to creases under his left eye.

'Aye, lass, I'm a Geordie.'

Sally wasn't sure if he was teasing her so she smiled uncertainly then laughed openly when he added.

'Just waitin' for the boat to come in.'

The word 'boat' was drawn out and sounded like a small foghorn.

Sally had not really spoken to any of the older members of staff before, other than on school matters. She was slightly nervous of them, as if they might think of her more like an overgrown sixth-former, which is how she felt and thought she must appear in their eyes. Mr Booth wore a navy blazer with silvery buttons and grey trousers and his shoes were highly polished. He definitely looked like a proper teacher.

'Well, I think we can go and get ourselves a cup of tea now. Just time before they shut up shop.'

Sally was relieved. She was not sure if break duty meant every single minute. It had done with one teacher. The staff room was still bustling. There was no queue for tea and Rita was behind the counter drying up cups and saucers. She smiled to see Mr Booth.

'You're late today Robert. I'd given up on you. Flapjack's all gone.'

'Pity.'

He spooned sugar into his cup and stirred briskly.

'Still, good news for the waistline, thanks, Rita.'

He turned, winked at Sally, and went to sit down in the geography department section. The whole staffroom was unofficially carved up into subject areas, like railway carriages; two rows of seats faced each other, separated by low tables.

The art department was sandwiched in between modern languages (where the head of French wore variations on the French flag, blue, white and red, in different configurations every day) and maths. A whole wall of windows looking out onto a variety of trees made it a light and pleasant room. Sally squeezed onto the edge of a shared chair with Carol, the pottery teacher.

'He's a bit of all right.'

'Who?'

'Him, Andy, over there, history teacher. Don't pretend you haven't noticed. I've seen you looking at him. You got all flustered yesterday when he spoke to you.'

'Was it that obvious?'

'Yeah, you went all red.' Carol turned to talk to another teacher. The room was stuffy and crowded and Sally felt fenced in squashed on the chair with Carol.

She put her cup on the table and frowned. It was so difficult controlling her feelings. Why couldn't she just keep it light hearted, talk easily like all the other teachers? How could she rid herself of this ridiculous intensity? She felt so tense she just couldn't relax or make small talk. How could she control the ridiculous blushing? She thought back to a particular tutorial at college where she had been so emotional and tongue-tied she was unable to speak. They had been discussing Chomsky and the acquisition of language. The lecturer read out a phrase that was considered meaningless in that each word cancelled the last: 'colourless green ideas sleep furiously'. Sally had been filled with confusion as she thought the phrase beautiful and it made perfect sense to her. She felt hot and awkward and unable to say anything. Another student eventually spoke up and calmly proclaimed 'but it's like poetry', a simple statement. Sally had also considered it poetry but had been in such an emotional turmoil she could not voice those thoughts. The anguish and intensity of that tutorial stayed with her, a reminder of how she needed to try and be calm and rational and put her emotions to one side, particularly when dealing with people. She still didn't find it easy. Carol turned to her again. Apparently, she had chatted to Andy last week and discovered he came from somewhere near Glasgow. He had joined the staff a year ago.

'So you don't need to worry. He's more or less a new boy like us.'

The bell rang and most of the teachers stood up, took their cups back to the hatch, picked up registers and left the room. Carol reached under her chair and put on a grey stained apron.

'Well, let's see if I can stop a few more of 3B chucking clay up onto the ceiling while my back's turned. See you later.'

Sally sat back and sipped her tea. She had a free period, and although she needed to clear up the mess in her art room due to her hasty departure for break duty, it could wait. The staffroom was more or less empty.

'OK if I sit here?'

She hadn't realised Andy was still in the room and she swallowed her tea nervously and hoped she wasn't blushing again. He introduced himself and told her he taught history then he asked her how she was finding the job, adding that he hadn't found it easy at first.

'It helps when you get to know the kids. I've only been here a year but you build up a relationship and they start to respect you. When I started, they all pretended they couldn't understand my accent and kept shouting for subtitles, the cheeky sods.'

Sally laughed.

Andy started to talk about Scotland. He visited his parents on the west coast fairly often and this gave him plenty of opportunities for painting landscapes. He asked Sally about her own art and after briefly explaining her degree work she mentioned the old house, her new home.

'I look out onto a heath so it's like a landscape within a city and there is so much sky and it's always changing.'

He seemed to dismiss this as an inferior suburban example of a landscape.

'You can't beat the islands for changing skies. Have you ever been to Jura?

Later that day Sally stood at the window of her room preparing to go out. Andy was an interesting possibility, she thought, as she stuck an earring through her lobe. She couldn't be sure what he thought of her. Her judgement of others' opinions had been shaken by her experience with Freddy.

Van Morrison filled the room and she had the music turned up to full volume. The white stereo was set up on a low table near the gas fire, where a box of LPs had burst open and spilled onto the floor. She carelessly pulled the needle from the record and turned off the one socket in the room. Her father had shuddered when he saw the wiring. In her ignorance, she saw the Bakelite plugs with their twisted flex as charming, part of the antique character of the house, while her father saw them as a positive menace. Picking up her bag, she sprayed perfume on her neck then ran down the three flights of stairs and out onto the heath to wait for the bus.

An increasing number of Sally's friends lived on an estate in Deptford where rents were cheap. Blocks of unmodernised 1930s and 1940s council flats had been let to so-called problem families but now the local authority was trying to mix in students, social workers, nurses and teachers. The 1930s flats had no heating other than a fireplace and no basin in the bathroom, just a deep sink in the kitchen. More flats, built in the 1940s, on the other side of the railway line, were slightly more luxurious, with a bathroom basin and a cupboard that blew out hot air and was called central heating. She'd been tempted to put her name down for a flat earlier in the summer but that had been before she visited the house on the heath.

Sally got off the bus at the Broadway opposite the old cinema and started walking down Deptford Church Street. The pavements felt greasy and the old apartment blocks that stood very close to the road looked like prisons. She turned off the main street and into the car park of Cathy's block of flats. As she climbed up two flights of stairs she turned onto the concrete balcony and could see her friends Cathy and Liz sitting outside on wicker chairs. It was an exotic scenario in such drab surroundings, an oasis of colour in so much grimness. Patchwork cushions sat on pink chairs, a basket of flowers hung from the door and a green wooden parrot swung from the supporting chain. On the kitchen windowsill stood three pots of geraniums.

'Hallo Sally, come and have a drink.'

Sally carried her beer and a stool out onto the balcony. Although the light was fading, between two buildings a few streaks of pink were visible. The main view from the flat was of the railway arches carrying the trains from London Bridge to Greenwich.

They discussed jobs, and Cathy asked Sally about her school and the missing girl. Liz said she had seen the photo on the telly and wasn't surprised that the search on Sunday had come to nothing. She waved her hand across the balcony.

'Look at all the lockups under the railway arches. There's loads of them and they stretch for miles. Imagine having to search all of them. Well, you couldn't. I've seen all sorts going in there, even a horse being shod last week.'

Sally looked up and smiled.

'It probably belongs to the tinkers who live down by the creek.'

Sally described how she had got lost one day as she was walking from Greenwich to Deptford and had taken a wrong turning off Creek Road. She had seen a cobbled track clogged with mud, squat huts with horses' heads looking out. There'd been a whole row of rag-and-bone men surrounded by piles of straw and carts of scrap metal. Sally was curious about horses in such an urban setting. She supposed the tinkers had been there for a good few years but had gradually been squeezed out. Much of the land along that part of the river was an uncertain mix of disused industrial buildings, chunks of cracked concrete and a dumping ground for bits of machinery and old cars. She wasn't sure how long the tinkers would stay but was glad she had seen them. It was another example of how living in this part of London could surprise you. No one would know they were there surviving on a thin strip of the past between the main road and the river.

The distinctive sound of a 2CV engine interrupted their conversation and a car pulled in and parked under their balcony. On the roof rack were a couple of surfboards, one cream and the other pale blue. They glowed like strange sea creatures in the gloomy evening light.

Cathy called to them. 'Hey Jeff, Angus, come and have a drink.'

Two faces looked up and were only really clearly visible when they smiled and their teeth showed white. The two young men had been in Cornwall for most of the summer and had returned for the last time, now the weather had changed, to collect all their kit before the winter.

They told stories of big waves, campfires and a life lived entirely outside. They had tasted many freedoms during the summer, a freedom from the usual English weather, a freedom from possessions, a freedom from responsibilities. Each new day had been as reliably sunny as the previous one and they felt both relaxed and as expansive as the endless sandy beach. Their experiences were on their faces, still tanned, their lips dry and hair long and bleached, small trails of sand under their feet. They both looked slightly wild and from another place.

After an hour or so the drink had run out and Jeff was yawning.

'Well, I'm knackered, got to go. Like a lift, Sally?

The thought of a lift was very attractive, since she didn't fancy hanging around at the bus stop now it was late.

Jeff eased the car out of the estate onto the dual carriageway.

'I can't believe I was in Cornwall this morning. It already seems a lifetime away. Actually, it is. This is really the end of being a student; no more long holidays, weeks of surfing and beaches. It feels all the more poignant because this summer has been so perfect. In fact, I'm starting to feel middle aged. I see a lifetime of drudgery before me. Twenty-three and already over the hill.'

Sally smiled. 'I've been in my job for a few weeks now and I feel so young and ignorant.'

'As long as the kids don't think that. You probably seem old enough to them. Is this where you live?'

The car stopped and Sally got out. Jeff pushed the flap of the window up with a snap.

'Maybe we can meet for a drink sometime, compare notes on being young and ignorant?"

'Yes, we could. Phone me. Thanks again.'

By the time Sally reached her room, she could just see Jeff's car in the distance with the surfboards skimming across the heath. She realised he didn't know her new phone number.

The next morning she woke early, having forgotten to close the curtains. The room was light. She couldn't get back to sleep and sat up in bed surveying her new room. The teaching files and register were stacked on the table under the window. It was not a comfortable room or one you felt like lingering in but the best thing about it was the view of the heath. Sally got out of bed and padded across the threadbare rug to the window where she leaned her arms on the sill. The expanse of green was peaceful at this time of day and the distant rectangles of houses were bright with the early morning sun.

She pushed her teaching files across the table and the register slipped off and onto the floor. It fell open and Sally flicked through the different classes. An empty column jumped out at her, a third-year group on a Wednesday afternoon. There was another one: her fourth-year group on a Tuesday. The dates were filled in at the top but the columns where the ticks for attendance should be were empty. She'd forgotten to take the registers at the start of the lessons, and had been so intent on getting everyone quiet and settled she'd omitted this important task. It was not something you could do in retrospect. She couldn't make it up and she couldn't remember who exactly was there as she barely knew all their names. Sally closed the book and wondered what, if anything, she should do. Should she tell anyone and if so what would be the point? Would anyone ask to see the registers?

Brushing her teeth at the basin near the open window, Sally heard the familiar sound of a 2CV. Looking out she saw it was Jeff and wondered what he was doing here so early. She leaned out and shouted 'I'll come down,' not wanting his knocking at the door to wake anyone or attract attention. Propping open the front door with an old brass lion, she stepped outside to meet him.

'I don't have your phone number. It's a beautiful day. I start work on Monday and I thought we should go to Brighton. I have a picnic in the car.'

Sally stood in her dressing gown taking in his unbrushed hair and the bottle of wine on the back seat.

He followed her eyes.

'Yes, well, we can get the food part of the picnic on the way.'

So they went.

The beach was almost empty and the holidaymakers long gone. It seemed too cold to swim but two children were playing at the water's edge with a plastic shark that had ridiculous eyebrows.

'Not exactly Jaws,' commented Jeff, which made Sally laugh, and she smiled as she thought of it during the day. They stayed on the beach, reading, eating and drinking, not talking very much but relaxed in each other's company. By early evening the place was almost deserted except for a lone dog walker. It became calmer and quieter as the sun sank lower in the sky, and you could hear the water on the shingle, rhythmic, like the sea quietly breathing.

Jeff started packing his bag. 'Well that's it. I declare the summer, the best summer of my life, finally over.

It can't be prolonged any more. I give in. I surrender myself to the autumn.' He stood up. 'Let's go.'

It was dark as they reached Blackheath. Jeff mentioned his new job and Sally's thoughts turned to her own and something she had put to the back of her mind surfaced again. It was the two empty columns in the class registers for the previous week. Perhaps she could ask all the pupils this week if they had been present the week before. Would they tell the truth?

Jeff broke into her thoughts.

'Do you know what I think we should do to finish off such a perfect day?'

'Tell me.'

'I think we should spend the night on that roof in your house. Who knows when we'll have the chance again.'

Sally didn't need much convincing. It seemed a logical conclusion to such a day of spontaneity.

Two hours later, after a couple of drinks, the two of them were muffling their giggles into the blankets they were struggling to push through the trap door to the roof. A particularly fat pillow was stuck at one point and Sally wobbled precariously on the ladder. It was at this moment she remembered the shark's eyebrows, lost control and nearly fell off onto the bathroom floor. Jeff was behind on the ladder and pushed her upwards. The two of them finally squashed through the square hole up to the flat space of the roof, still giggling.

'Oh, I forgot to bring a torch.' Sally threw the blankets and sleeping bags on top of the pillows.

She was reluctant to go down again and unsure about any unwritten rules of the house. Reg had not mentioned anything about friends staying the night. Sally quietly shut the trap door to the bathroom, making a mental note that she should check before opening it in the morning in case anyone was having a bath or using the toilet. No one need know they were there.

A voice came out of the blackness.

'It's not that dark. Your eyes get used to it, like the cinema. Come and lie down. We can look at the stars.'

PAMELA

I have a friend. He is a boy so I could say I have a boyfriend but he is just a friend. He is interested in me and asks about my home, my family and knows I am desperate to have a dog. Caroline and I went to the pet shop again on Saturday. We were in there for ages and I was looking at all the puppies and deciding which one to buy if only my mum would let me. I chose a border collie, black and white with such lovely eyes. It kept looking at me in such a sad way as if it was begging me to take it away from the small cage in the pet shop and let it run free in the park. I thought how the puppy and me would go home for tea and she could lay in front of the fire and later creep into my bedroom and curl up on my bed even though she would have a cosy cushion in her basket. I don't know why my mum won't let me have a dog. It's not fair. Loads of people in our flats have them. The boy who is my friend wants a dog too but his mum won't let him either. He waits for me after school sometimes and has walked with me as far as the shops. I think I can tell him anything. I still have my old friends and they sometimes tease me about him but I can tell they admire me because they think he's a boyfriend and they would like to have a boyfriend for themselves. I feel a bit more grown up now because he is four years older and has dark brown hair and a nice smile. He told me if anyone gives me any bother I should tell him and he will sort them out. That makes me feel safe. I think he lives near me. He hasn't told me exactly where but I think it's one of those new blocks near the park. My mum doesn't know about him and I won't tell her because she won't like it and she would think he might 'try it on'. I know he won't. He's not like that. He is my friend and I like him, he likes me and we like chatting together especially about dogs. I don't know why out of all the girls in the school he talks to me but he does. He has chosen me. It makes me feel special.

October

WILSON

Wilson wasn't looking forward to searching the tunnels. How many times had he requested that the council board up the entrances properly? Kids were always breaking in. It wasn't difficult. As a kid himself Wilson had heard rumours that a train full of passengers got stuck inside one of the tunnels and had been bricked in. Even at the tender age of seven he had found this unlikely but it unsettled him nevertheless.

Ever since the railway line had been closed in the early 1950s the tunnels had been a constant nuisance, frequented by tramps, kids and hooligans. The grand but lumbering old railway station had survived in an increasingly derelict state until 1960. One of Wilson's cousins, a Teddy Boy and slightly older, had persuaded him to look around the old station one day while they were waiting for a bus on their way back from the cinema. Spurred on by the anarchy and violence in the film, Wilson and his cousin kicked in a couple of rotten doors and threw some bricks through already smashed windows. It was a futile exercise as the station was already beyond repair with half the roof gone, torn pigeon nets flapping in the wind, and broken benches in the unwelcoming waiting rooms. It had been Wilson's only excursion into vandalism, egged on by his older cousin, but he had felt just a small amount of guilt at inflicting more damage to a building that was so obviously doomed.

There were two tunnels. Paxton Tunnel was the one nearest to the Crystal Palace station and they started at the south portal. It was a dismal sight, with overgrown shrubs hanging over the entrance and bits of splintered boxes strewn about. The prefabs behind them were more or less abandoned now and awaiting demolition, which added to the air of despondency. The keys to the wooden doors were obviously redundant. Someone had smashed and splintered the wood with an axe, leaving a jagged hole so that anyone could enter.

The dogs were straining on their leads and the policemen controlling them were equally anxious to get this over with. It was a gusty day with a fine rain that blew on the wind like soft needles and the tunnels offered a gloomy sort of shelter. The group of three policemen, two with dogs now let off their leads, trudged through the darkness with thin lines of light from their torches. The tunnel was not straight; it curved through the difficult gradient, so no light was visible until you almost reached the end. The dogs darted away into unseen recesses, sniffing the sooty brickwork. Evidence of recent occupation was just visible in the form of a sleeping bag and a few empty beer bottles. It was a damp fruitless search and brought them out at the other end onto a five-a-side pitch in a small park, deserted and bare in the drizzle. They dutifully secured the doors of the tunnel – a pointless exercise, knowing it wasn't difficult to gain access at either end.

As the police constable fumbled with the keys, Wilson lit a cigarette. He thought of his Aunt Lily as he frequently did whenever he visited the tunnels. During the war she was always popping round to their house with news of the latest air raid damage. Surely she had mentioned sheltering in a tunnel up at Crystal Palace? Apparently there had been musicians there, soup was served and people stayed the night in bunk beds. As a child, he thought it sounded good fun, like a party almost, and certainly preferable to the shelter his father had built next to the shed. They often had to sleep there despite the water-logged floor. He had never been certain which tunnel his Aunt Lily meant, but it stayed in his mind as a jolly alternative to the gloomy shelter in the garden. He remembered the description because as a young lad he was still intrigued by the story of the bricked-up train. It was one of many half-understood conversations he was always overhearing as a boy.

He had been woken on countless occasions at all times of night and dragged, bleary-eyed, down to the cold garden. His whole childhood seemed to be one of interruptions. Aged six, his small old-fashioned infant school was replaced with a far rougher place when they moved house. At eight he had been sent to an aunt in Kent as an evacuee. It hadn't lasted. Just as he was settling to the strange smelling house and slow rural school, his mother came and yanked him back. Apparently, she missed him. The bricked-up train story became connected in his mind with air raids and shelters, collapsing buildings and being trapped. A boy in his class had been buried under the bricks of his own house after a direct hit one night. His desk remained empty for a few days and then it was removed. As a child in London during the war, Wilson's sense of claustrophobia was heightened and left him with a fear of being shut in, blocked or buried, with no means of escape. He would always associate Aunt Lily with these tunnels and wished he had spoken to her about them, but now it was too late. She had died ten years ago.

Outside the southern portal of Crescent Wood Tunnel the land was bare and flat. Blocks of flats towered above the railway bridge behind a few thin trees. There was a circle of black where a recent fire had been lit on the grass. Empty cans of glue were scattered around some upturned boxes. Wilson was totally baffled by this latest craze for kids to 'get their kicks'. He understood alcohol, less so the smoking of cannabis, but sniffing glue was beyond him, though it was becoming increasingly common. Those kids with spiky hair causing havoc in shopping centres, acting in an exaggerated and threatening manner, scaring old people and leering at mothers with children were like a breed apart. He kicked the cans into the bushes. There was nothing doing here. The tunnels were empty. He would write to the council again requesting that they secure the doors properly. No doubt he'd receive the same reply, that they would look into it, then nothing would happen. It didn't seem to be a priority.

STANLEY

The boy came again today. He's been hanging around for a while. He likes Bessie and sits and strokes her and talks to her quietly. He asked if he could take her for a walk. I didn't see why not. It helps me out as I don't feel like going far these days. I think the silly bitch is going to have puppies. It certainly looks that way. God knows what I'll do with them. Get rid of them I suppose. I could do without the bother. I don't feel up to much recently. Off my food and so tired. I might ask the boy to go to the shops for me. Just have to trust him with the money. I don't want to ask that nosey old bat in the prefab, she might start trying to help out again. Not on your nelly.

The boy says he wants a puppy but he's not allowed. Well, they'll have to go, no room for them here. There's enough that needs seeing to without having to bother with puppies. I feel so tired. Why do I feel so tired? I hope the boy comes tomorrow.

ALAN

In preparation for the railway project, Alan visited the local history library. It had been a convent sometime in the recent past and retained a serenity in the clean tiled floor and the dark polished wood of the stair treads. A young woman helped him with maps and newspaper cuttings, smiling at his enthusiasm when he found photos of some of the old railway stations. Alan had been tempted to ask her if she fancied a cup of tea, maybe the café at the Standard, but thought better of it. Leaving the library, he had called in at the art gallery downstairs. A young woman with dark curly hair was standing in front of a large landscape painting. She turned to Alan and grinned. 'It's sold, my painting has a red dot, can you believe it?'

He could. It was colourful and expressive. Her excitement was infectious and he enthused about her work while registering her brown eyes and full mouth. As she left in search of a phone box to contact her mum, she stopped in the doorway and turned to wave. As he raised his hand in response, his mind took a photo of her, smiling and waving framed by the door with the light from the window on her face.

Walking back down through the park Alan felt optimistic. The visit had been useful. He now had a clear idea of the whole track from Greenwich to Crystal

Palace and several photos showing some of the stations. The fleeting encounters with two young women had boosted his confidence and suddenly many things seemed possible.

He had to admit to himself that he was lonely. Fiona had been his only girlfriend. It would be too easy to back-pedal into that relationship. It had taken a long time to extricate himself and there should be no going back. For two years at university they had been together for different reasons. He had wanted a companion, someone to visit galleries with, go for a drink or talk over the day. She had wanted someone to be seen with, someone to accompany her to the theatre, an arm to hang onto. In the beginning, it had worked well. He first met her at one of the college dances. A sparkling presence in pale turquoise, she had accidently on purpose spilled her drink onto his sleeve, a very bold action on her behalf he found out later, but just as well because he would never have had the courage to talk to her otherwise.

So they had become Fiona and Alan, a couple, and they were invited to meals with other couples. They occasionally met Rob and Alison for a drink, which was a bit more lively, as Rob openly teased Fiona, something she seemed to enjoy at first, and Alison had a good sense of humour.

Sex had been a bit awkward in the early days but Fiona had finally granted him access to her body as a reward for being a good boyfriend. It felt rather like being awarded a Scout badge.

It became apparent to Alan that he and Fiona had different ideas of where their relationship was going. He saw it as a springboard, a taster, before exploring other avenues; she saw it as a prelude to marriage, a safety net within which to be a wild student (wildness being the spilling of a drink on a strange man's arm), an experiment before they settled down to safe, suffocating sensibleness. It had taken longer than he thought to end the relationship, as other events had got in the way, but it was well and truly over now. He was a free man, wasn't he?

Later that day Alan had only just got changed when the doorbell rang. He leaped up the stairs two at a time and was surprised to see Fiona. How did she know his new address?

'Hallo Alan, I've brought you a flat warming present.'

Alan stood uncertainly in the doorway. He was wearing a pair of old running shorts, and had just opened a bottle of beer before settling down to watch television. He was reluctant to ask her in as she had never seen his flat, and he liked this. Her ignorance of his current living accommodation kept her firmly in the past where he wanted her to stay. Not to ask her in though would seem rude, and particularly when she had brought a present, but he felt manipulated all the same, and resentful.

'You'd better come in.'

He followed her perfume down the stairs and, needing the protection of clothing, picked up a pullover from the banister.

'So, can you show me the flat?'

'Not much to see really. This is the kitchen. Would you like a drink? I'm just having a beer.'

'Do you have any squash? I'm in the Mini.'

She put the wrapped parcel on the draining board where the tissue paper immediately soaked up a puddle of water.

'Go on, open it.'

It was a wooden salad bowl with two carved spoons nestling neatly inside. The grain made swirling patterns.

'I thought it might be useful with the weather we had this summer. You don't have one already do you?'

'No, I don't. Thank you, it's very attractive, stylish. Thank you.'

'So, is this the sitting room? Oh, Alan, it's very bare. Did you cut the legs off that table?'

'Yes, I wanted it low.'

'A dinky bathroom. Not sure about the lemon walls, but I guess you can paint them.'

'Yes, I plan to.

Was it his imagination or did she stand a little too close to him in the hallway, waiting for him to grab her, tell her he found her irresistible? Well, it wasn't going to happen.

'And the bedroom?'

She was sensitive enough to wait for Alan to open the door This was the room he least wanted her to see. It was a reminder that they had once shared a bed.

'Oh, are you covering up the smell of anything?'

Fiona pointed to the milk bottle containing three joss sticks on the window sill. She meant it as a risqué little joke, showing she knew about drugs. He found it intensely irritating and the tone of his answer showed this very clearly.

'Yes, damp.'

She understood she was not wanted and said in a quiet voice.

'I should go. Perhaps I shouldn't have come in the first place.'

Alan didn't contradict her but thanked her again for the bowl, although he wasn't sure he would ever use it, particularly now that summer was over. It seemed a useless suburban object somehow symbolic of their relationship. Fiona almost ran up the stairs and out onto the open heath leaving his front door wide open. He shut it and returned to his beer and television, annoyed that she had disturbed him and made him feel so guilty.

Alan and Rob started the railway visits that Sunday. It hadn't taken long to reach the site of the first station – Greenwich Park. This was where the antique market now stood on the car park opposite the garage. It was Sammy Tyler, a friend from Alan's market days and a dealer in furniture of dubious origin, who had told him about the old railway station on the same site that had been pulled down several years earlier. He and Alan would stand together in the market, stamping their feet in the cold, hands round mugs of sweet tea. If Sammy was in the mood he could be quite informative.

'Yeah, my mate used the old station as a builders' yard, had it since the 1930s. Full of rats it was.'

Sammy would have a continual roll-up held inwards in the palm of his hand, a First World War habit from the trenches apparently, though Alan wasn't sure if Sammy had actually fought. Most of his stories had to be taken with a pinch of salt. He had been right about the station though.

Alan took several photos of the market site showing St Alphege's as a point of reference. He nodded to most of the stallholders and noticed a man selling comics on what had been his old pitch. Rob had wandered over to a young woman selling Victorian lace.

Alan pulled a photo out of his pocket from the local history library showing a side view of the old station with a wooden canopy on which GREENWICH PARK had been hand painted. A whole row of buildings fronted onto the road where the market stalls now stood. The single-storey station was in the middle, and on either side were two- or three-storey buildings with shops below and flats above. From the backs of these houses there would have been an excellent view of the station platforms and the track. Alan imagined the steam billowing up and obscuring the view from a dingy bedroom where someone in a nightgown might have stood. He would have loved a room in such a house and might have set up a table by the window where he could sit drinking tea looking down at the trains arriving and departing on the platform below.

Alan and Rob walked away from the market along the rough line of what they considered had been the railway track and stopped opposite a flower shop. According to the map, the track would have crossed the road here and disappeared behind this building.

They leaned their bikes against a fence and Rob took off his hat.

'I was here last night. I had a few drinks round the corner and passed here on my way home.'

'Yeah, we've both passed here loads of times. There must have been a bridge or the track would have run under the road.'

'But listen to me, Alan. I was here last night and I found a sort of alleyway at the side of that building.'

Alan didn't ask what Rob had been doing in this exact spot the previous evening. He knew that Rob made it his business to familiarise himself with every available secret area in the vicinity. Behind the shops and wine bars seen from the street were centuries of rearranging and altering. An old bake house extended into a kitchen or stables incorporated into a restaurant. He knew all the hidden courtyards, the covered passageways and blocked up doorways. They had made use of some of these short cuts on their way back from the pub many a time.

Alan followed Rob as he pushed through a half open gate and they passed along a high brick wall on one side and a cliff of concrete on the other. This led to a scruffy courtyard packed haphazardly with old crates.

These proved useful for climbing on to see over the high fence.

'Wow, look at that.'

Alan was the first to clamber up and stood wobbling as he struggled with his camera and wedged his elbows between the slats of wood to steady himself. At first he thought he saw a track, but his imagination was filling that in; he only really saw the curve where the track had been. The curve led to what was unmistakably a signal box that stood like a small medieval castle, marooned behind rows of thin Victorian houses.

Focusing his camera, he took several shots of the signal box, then zoomed in. One of the windows was broken and the steps leading up looked rotten, but the building itself was beautifully intact. Although he took more photos, it was that first view that imprinted itself on his brain, visual proof that the railway still existed there over a hundred years later.

Rob briefly peered over the fence. 'Shall we have a coffee somewhere?'

'Already? We've only just started. Let's go to the next station – it's not far.'

'So, which way?'

Rob leaned against his bike, or more correctly Alison's bike, with a weary expression.

Alan wondered again what Rob had been up to the previous evening but he thought he probably knew. Rob seemed to pre-empt a question that had not actually been asked but was in Alan's mind.

'Alison has gone away for the weekend visiting her parents. A family gathering of some sort.'

'It seems a bit shabby, going behind her back.'

'What the head doesn't know, the heart doesn't grieve.'

'Don't escape into clichés.'

Rob looked down at his feet resting on the pavement either side of the pedals.

Alan knew Rob wouldn't want to hurt Alison. They had been together for several years, ran a successful business, and their relationship worked on many levels. But still Rob seemed to need the spice of extra conquests.

'It's all froth, quite addictive I suppose but also fairly temporary. I can't imagine I will have the energy for it once I hit forty.'

Rob looked directly at Alan.

'Nobody knows about any of this except you, and I trust you to be discreet.'

'Of course. I wouldn't want to upset Alison.'

They didn't speak as they pedalled towards Blackheath Hill, the second station on the line. The building was recognisable from the front on the road but more interesting when they snooped around the back. An old Bedford van was parked under an archway that would previously have been a tunnel taking the track under the road. The tunnel was more or less filled in and the site obviously used as some sort of builders' yard. Lengths of scaffolding and bits of metal were strewn around in random piles. Alan spoke to the owner of the Bedford van who was quite surly at first but gradually thawed out when he realised they were not the police and just wanted stories of the station.

He told them the station had closed round about the end of the first war, just before he was born. It had been used as a billiard hall and his dad used to come and play there in the 1920s. He wasn't sure when they rebuilt it, as he was living down in Deptford by then. The original station was all wood and there were still bits of it knocking about. He had come back about eight years ago when his dad popped his clogs and his mum retired from the bakery

'Yeah, yeah, you can take photos. Just let me move my van out of your way first.'

SALLY

Sally came down to the kitchen where Reg was preparing cooked breakfasts. The smell of fat hung heavy in the air.

'Good morning. The usual?'

'Please.'

Reg filled the teapot then covered it with a woollen hat that was crusty and brown around the hole for the spout. Stubbing out his cigarette, he put a small black frying pan on the gas and flicked a piece of white lard into it, which melted immediately. His movements were comical and jerky. He attempted humour to cover up his arthritis but it wasn't always clear where one finished and the other began, not even to Reg himself. Comedy was his way of dealing with his ageing body. In a house full of young 'stoodents' he didn't want to feel ridiculous.

He flipped the crispy bacon out of the pan onto two pieces of white bread then squeezed a plastic tomato in the general direction of the plate, the sauce covering it in a big red scribble. This was his breakfast and the plate was set aside under the eye level grill as he prepared Sally's poached egg.

Returning to the stove he tipped a tin of tomatoes into a saucepan.

'Something for the vegetarians.'

The next minute he had picked up the bacon pan and was pouring the remaining fat into the tomatoes.

'Give it a bit of taste.'

Sally concentrated on her breakfast, smiling to herself, as one of the vegetarians came into the room and sat opposite her.

Thirty minutes later she was sitting on the top deck of a bus somewhere between Blackheath and Crystal Palace, her bag of teaching files on the seat beside her. The traffic was building up and they seemed to be stuck on a one-way system just outside Catford. Sally smiled at the seemingly contradictory title 'Catford dog racing stadium' on the poster by the railway station.

The traffic seemed to thin and the bus started to move faster away from the shops and up a hill, passing a little newsagent's squashed into the corner. It stopped and a woman with a pushchair got on. Sally suddenly recognised exactly where they were. She had bought a pint of milk in that shop one Sunday morning over a year ago while staying in Freddy's flat. Sally realised with dismay that the tall Victorian house where Freddy had lived was gone; a whole row of houses had been pulled down and the area was boarded up for redevelopment. As the bus pulled away Sally looked back at the vast space created; the mid-Victorian mansions had had very generous gardens and with their frontier of buildings removed provided a huge area for new housing. Over one hundred years of planting shrubs, mowing lawns, cutting roses, sitting outside wooden summer-houses bleached by the sun, had all been bulldozed and covered in rubble. Sally felt sad thinking both of the destroyed houses and of Freddy. His flat had been two rooms at the top of the four-storey house, five if you included the basement. The toilet was on the floor below and there had been a small gas stove squashed onto the landing outside the sitting room. She had to admit on reflection it had seemed dangerous cooking in such a high-up tiny confined space. Freddy had grilled some lamb chops, the fat spitting wildly, then boiled some potatoes with peas and even made gravy. Sally had been touched at the effort made, cooking what, for students, seemed like a slightly old-fashioned meal. Other friends would have made spaghetti Bolognese, something easier to cope with on a two-burner stove. The flat had been so cold. They slept under five blankets with coats piled on top.

She had liked Freddy but came to think of him as a feather. He was always floating around, often stoned. He would appear in the lecture theatre, or the bar, not stay long, then just disappear. She would see the back of him, slim hips, slightly broader shoulders, long brown hair falling to one side, walking through the library. When she looked up again he had gone. He was a gentle, dreamy person with a sharp intellect, smiling in an affable, probably weed-induced way at the world. Their relationship had sort of petered out. Nothing definite was said. He just didn't come to visit her room in the hall of residence any more, didn't seek her out in the cafeteria or bar.

She understood it was over but wasn't sure why.

Two weeks later she saw him with a drama student who wore scarves tied in a band around her head. She seemed the kind of person who was always in the middle of things, laughing easily with lots of people in the bar. Sally wondered what she had done wrong. Was it her awkwardness when groups of friends sat around smoking dope and she took a pretend puff and passed it on? Was it her inability to make small talk or the fact that she took everything people said literally that had put him off?

'God, you are so gullible Sal,' he had once said quite aggressively and she was struck dumb and could only blush. She felt hurt by the lack of communication but came to accept that she was not a very good judge of character.

It was strange to think of being in Freddy's flat that no longer existed, of sleeping about thirty foot above the ground in a room that was no longer there. She saw herself eating lamb chops sitting cross-legged on a floor surrounded by LP covers and ashtrays. Now it was gone and only existed in her memory.

Where was Freddy now?

A loud voice broke into her thoughts. The bus had stopped on another hill.

'You two, yes, you, put your hats on immediately or I'll report you.'

A plumpish woman had stood up and was shouting out of the small open upper window to two girls standing below at the bus stop.

Sally saw they were outside a school. She didn't know which one, but judging by the uniform and the fairly docile groups of girls, it looked posh. The plump woman was bustling off the bus, pushing the groups of girls with hats and brown satchels in front of her.

'Come along, come along, don't dilly dally.'

The bus pulled away and continued to climb the hill, finally reaching the plateau that was Crystal Palace. As she got off, Sally spoke sternly to herself.

'Don't you ever become the sort of embarrassing teacher who shouts at pupils in public.'

She decided to walk along Crystal Palace Parade instead of taking a second bus. The road was high here and layers of London skyline stretched into the distance and there was space on the right where the Palace would have been. To the left was a long brick wall that bordered a large sunken area much lower than the road. One end of this land had prefabs with a few cars parked and the other was a mixture of dumped household objects; mattresses and a couple of fridges. Sally noticed a caravan parked among the debris and briefly wondered if anyone lived in it. What was this strange dip in the land? It puzzled her. Looking at her watch Sally realised she might be late and started to run.

WILSON

Wilson sat at the desk in the old geography room at the school and took a gulp from a cup of cold coffee that had slopped in the saucer and half drowned a digestive biscuit. One of the school secretaries had hastily brought it to him at the end of break. It seemed rude not to drink it so he took another small sip, cursing as a few drips fell onto his tie.

From his makeshift desk he could see across the playground at the side of the school to the gate where Pamela Webb had last been seen.

The description of her last sighting he knew off by heart: 11-year-old girl, 5ft tall with reddish brown hair and dark brown eyes, wearing a light blue anorak with a fur trimmed hood, a navy blue skirt and jumper and blue and red striped tie, white knee socks and black shoes. She was carrying a pink plastic rucksack and waiting by the gate.

So far he had not been able to establish if she was alone. It had been lunchtime and officially children were not allowed off the premises unless they had permission to go home. This rule was proving difficult to enforce and the headmaster was considering making it compulsory to stay in school all day. But on that day, in September, there had been a straggle of children leaving the school at lunchtime, some legitimately and some not. Pamela did not have permission and as a new pupil in the school it was unusual to be breaking rules so early.

A knock on the door brought him back to the present. Miss Lloyd, the senior mistress, escorted a sniffing little girl into the room and indicated she sit opposite Wilson. He looked up and gave her what he hoped was a reassuring smile as he confirmed her name.

'How long have you known Pamela?'

'She was my best friend since infant school and we live on the same estate.'

The girl looked down as her nose started to run and she wiped it with the back of her hand.

'Did you come to school together?'

'Yes, most days, but not that day. I mean the day she disappeared.'

'Why not.'

'Because she was late. We're supposed to meet outside the newsagent's at half past. My mum said if she doesn't turn up by twenty to I must go. I waited till quarter to, then I ran so I wouldn't get late detention.'

'You saw her later though, at school?'

'Yes, at break she was standing by the toilets. I didn't speak to her.'

'Was she with someone?'

'I don't know. There were lots of kids. I don't know.' Her voice was a bit shaky, and she swallowed hard then wiped her nose again. The senior mistress gave her a sympathetic smile and nodded her head slightly as if encouraging her to carry on.

'There were loads of kids but I saw a big boy and girl standing nearby.'

'What were they doing?'

'Nothing, they were just standing there. Everyone else was rushing about, pushing along the corridor or going in or out of the toilets but they were just standing there. That's why I remember them.'

Wilson assured the girl that her information was useful and Miss Lloyd leaned forward and spoke directly to the policeman as she pushed a folded piece of paper across the table.

'Here are the names of the pupils we've identified.'

'Thank you, Miss Lloyd. One last question, Caroline. Did you see Pamela again that day?'

'No, she's not in my class and she wasn't in the dinner queue and I didn't see her in the playground either. We sometimes walk home together but not always. I went on the bus with Michelle and Stella that day.'

As the girl left the room, her duffle bag bumped against the doorframe. She turned to look at the policeman and he found it hard to read the expression on her face; it was a mixture of apprehension and weariness but behind that a glint of something harder. He didn't know what to call it, but it registered like a small stone in his mind.

Miss Lloyd stood up.

'The girl Caroline mentioned is waiting outside. Her name is Sharon. Would you like a short break or do you want to see her now?'

The girl sat opposite him, her hands with bitten fingernails clenched tightly on the desk, her face covered with thick make-up in an attempt to disguise the spots underneath. They still showed as pink bumps. She was attractive in a mean sort of way. Her dark eyes were lined heavily with black, the lashes stiff with mascara. Her lips were slightly dry with a smear of whitish lipstick and her dyed black hair hung straight as a ribbon just touching her shoulders. It may have been the make-up that helped give the impression of a mask, but her face was completely expressionless.

'Do you know Pamela Webb?'

The girl sat back slightly and relaxed her hands, spreading her fingers on the table. She looked Ray straight in the eye, and kept looking at him as she answered.

'I know who she is.'

'How well do you know her? Is she a friend?'

Her expressionless face softened slightly into faint ridicule at the suggestion of someone like her being friends with an eleven-year-old girl.

'From the estate, her flat is near mine.'

She continued to stare directly at him. The strength of her gaze was a sort of insolence and the force of it made her seem more like a woman of twenty-five than a schoolgirl of fifteen. Ray looked down at his notes more as a break from her glare than a need to check facts.

'Did you speak to her? Were you on talking terms?'

'I have spoken to her a few times.'

Her white school blouse was stretched tightly across her rounded breasts, a black bra clearly visible beneath the thin white fabric, the pink flesh spilling over the top.

'Did you speak to her on Monday 25th September, the day she went missing?'

'Can't remember.'

'You were seen standing near her at break, in the corridor, near the toilets so I just wondered if you said anything to her.'

'I don't think so. Why should I talk to her?'

'Who was the boy you were with?'

'Must have been Nick.'

'Did you see her later that day, perhaps at lunchtime, or in the afternoon?'

'I don't think so. I can't remember.'

'Or maybe you saw her in the evening near your flats?'

'I don't think so. I can't remember.'

'Do you have any information about Pamela that you think might help us? Do you know who her friends were or where she would play near the flats, anything at all?

For the first time she dropped her gaze and looked down at her hands on the table before answering.

'No, I don't.'

'Are you friendly with Nick?'

'Yes.'

'Is he friends with Pamela?'

'I don't think so, but why don't you ask him?'

Wilson told her she and Nick had been seen standing in a corridor near Pamela on the day she had disappeared. Sharon said they often met in that particular spot and no she hadn't been aware of Pamela being there. And that was it. Wilson issued the usual instructions to the girl before she left, telling her to contact him if she remembered anything else. He didn't think anything would come of it.

'Well, she's a tough one.' He turned to the senior mistress.

'Yes indeed. She comes from a difficult family and hasn't had an easy time at home. She seems so much older than her years, always has. She joined us at thirteen. Her family had moved from the Midlands. There were rumours they were gypsies or at least the father was. She settled in fairly quickly and made friends with Nick right from the start. She doesn't seem to have many friends apart from him, no girlfriends, and she doesn't hang around in groups or with anyone else in particular.'

'Is she bright?'

'Not in an academic sense. I think her schooling has been too interrupted, so she might sound confident when you speak to her but her writing is weak and she has a low reading age.'

Miss Lloyd had been consulting a beige foolscap folder, so she returned the papers to a pile and tapped them on the table to straighten them. She then passed a photo to Wilson.

The serious face of a younger Sharon looked directly at him. She appeared outwardly hostile and defiant but at the same time there was a hint of anxiety.

Miss Lloyd continued talking, telling Wilson that Sharon was responsible for looking after things at home like cooking and caring for the younger children. Apparently the father was not around much and the mother worked odd hours. 'She hasn't been in any trouble in her time here, well not serious trouble, although there was a period last year when she retaliated against some name-calling, but that seems to have stopped.'

Miss Lloyd sat back in her chair, the grey jacket of her suit falling open slightly to reveal a silky cream blouse with a well-pressed collar. She crossed her legs and there was a faint swooshing sound of nylon as her thick stockings brushed against each other. Her shoes were polished like conkers.

'What sort of name-calling?'

'I think it was to do with gypsies, but unfortunately I don't know the details. Sharon's house mistress, Valerie Jones, has more information, and she is also Pamela Webb's house mistress so I assume you would like to interview her.'

'And the boy, Nick, is he waiting outside?'

Miss Lloyd opened the door. 'Oh, he's not here but I'll see if I can find him. He can't have gone far.'

Wilson bit the end of his pen and looked out of the window into the playground that was rapidly filling up with children let out for lunch break. Some of the younger boys swooped and turned like leaves in the strong wind. He thought briefly of his own children possibly chasing leaves in a primary school playground not far away. Rosamund, at nine, was confident and slightly argumentative, Richard, at six was a joker and stubborn as an ox. Were they safe?

'Just go in, Nick, and take a seat opposite Detective Inspector Wilson, at the desk.'

Miss Lloyd resumed her position like an old-fashioned secretary about to take shorthand, her glasses reflecting the windows as two miniature rectangles of light.

'Sorry to hold you up, Inspector. Nick heard the lunch bell and assumed we were all taking a break so was heading for the dining hall.'

Nick smiled at Ray. He had a soft, round face framed with longish brown hair, his eyes were dark, almost black, and his skin was what Ray's mother would have described as ruddy.

'It's chips today. There's always a longer queue. I try to get there early. Do you want to ask me about Pamela?'

ALAN

It was a bright Saturday morning and Alan's shop had been open for two hours. The traffic outside was busy, the pavements full of people, and Alan had already sold three prints and two old maps. He opened the third drawer of the plan chest and, as it slid out smoothly, congratulated himself on the fine layer of beeswax he had applied to the wood.

'We have quite a few prints of Greenwich Park, across several centuries, many from the nineteenth century, but there are others. Have a look through these.'

He lifted a pile of mounts wrapped in cellophane onto the top of the plan chest and, as he stood back to give the customer more room, the doorbell from the front of the shop rang noisily. He automatically looked up and was surprised to see his mother standing there. She gave him a little wave then shrugged her shoulders as if to say don't let me interrupt your work, and started to sort through a box of old postcards. Alan felt he should stay with the customer in case he had any questions so he looked across at his mother from a distance, appraising her clothes.

This was an old habit. As a child he came to associate her different moods with the clothes she wore. He remembered being with her in the garden as a child, pulling up potatoes and snapping green beans. He had a small green metal wheelbarrow and black Wellington boots and she would hand him a biscuit from a tartan tin, which he ate sitting on the garden bench, his short legs swinging. She sat on the kitchen step and smoked, happy and relaxed in an old coat of his father's and a woollen bobble hat. The garden clothes meant working together. In the summer she would bring him lemon barley water in a glass with an image of a budgerigar, half scratched off. She wore ankle socks and brown lace-up shoes, sometimes a skirt and sometimes a different skirt that was really shorts in disguise, with a blouse and button-up cardigan. When she took the cardigan off while digging he noticed wet patches under the arms.

He learned to read her state of mind depending on her clothes. On rare occasions in the evening she wore a swooshy kind of dress that showed the top of her bosoms and plunged to a V-shape at the back. The material was crackly and slightly shiny. She always wore a necklace with earrings to match and shoes with a heel the same shape as the lavatory bowl. He was allowed to watch while she sat at her dressing table and went through what he came to think of as her 'dabbings'.

She dabbed powder on her nose, a little on the forehead, cheeks and chin, then she dabbed red lipstick on her lips in a slightly aggressive manner and the final dab was two drops of perfume behind her ears. Alan knew she was nervous in these clothes, as she never sat comfortably, always on the edge of any seat, breathing in short sighs as if her life had become more restrictive with her clothes. She would bite her lip and traces of the red lipstick would catch on her teeth, then she would jump up and smooth creases from the rustly material or quickly brush the fallen ash of a cigarette from her lap. She was never at ease in these clothes or any of the social situations that required her to wear them.

Alan was jolted out of his reverie by the customer moving.

He had propped the print against the wall and was standing back to get a better view.

'I think this is the best one. Yes, definitely. I like it. Can I pay by cheque?'

Alan and his mother sat in the window of a café. Tom, the man who ran the main shop, was minding Alan's section for ten minutes.

'The thing is, darling, I need your advice.' She lit a cigarette and held it close to her face with her eyes half closed against the smoke.

'It's Peggy.'

His body tensed slightly at the name, an involuntary response, even after all these years.

His mother spoke quickly, explaining that Peggy's mother had died recently and as a consequence her house and all its contents needed to be sold. They would really appreciate it if Alan would come and look over all the antiques and pictures to give a rough idea of the value.

'Peggy doesn't have a clue and is afraid some cowboy might come in and undervalue everything.'

Alan promised his mother he would visit her and Peggy the following Sunday afternoon. It would give him time to visit the third railway site in the morning then he would jump on a train and get this chore over and done with.

As he locked the shop later that afternoon Alan decided to walk along the river before going home. He breathed deeply as he faced the water, and noticed the tide was high. His thoughts returned to his mother and also Peggy as he turned to follow the path downstream.

His first memory of Peggy had been one lunchtime in summer when he was about six years old. He had come running in from the garden, blinking his eyes from the midday sun, and there she was, sitting at the kitchen table with a cup and saucer in front of her next to the shell ashtray. His mother saw him eyeing up a plate of custard creams.

'We are having lunch soon Alan. This is my friend Peggy. We knew each other in the war.'

'Hallo.'

'Hallo Alan. I had to take two buses to get here today. Do you like going on buses?'

He didn't know if he liked buses or not but he did like custard creams. He stared as his mother whisked the plate away and put the biscuits back in the tin. It seemed he was expected to speak.

'Were you fighting?'

'What do you mean? Oh, I see, the war.' Peggy threw back her head and laughed loudly. Alan saw she had a gold tooth and thought she was a bit frightening.

'No, we were working on the land, helping the farmers, growing the food. I used to drive a tractor.'

This time Alan was impressed.

'Oh, was it red like mine?'

It was one of his favourite toys. He would plough up fields endlessly across the living room carpet.

'Do you know, I can't remember. Can you, Jean?'

His mother smiled at him and Peggy.

'No, I can't. In my memory, it was just rusty and covered in mud so brown is the only colour that springs to mind.'

Peggy had visited several times after that, always in the day when his father was at work, although Alan had thought nothing of it; she was just one of the small circle of his mother's friends.

Alan briefly sat on a bench and watched a toddler throwing crusts to a seagull. More seagulls appeared, and he stood up and carried on walking along the river path. His thoughts turned again to Peggy and to that most upsetting of moments in his childhood.

His parents were arguing a lot at that time, and his father would come home from work, irritable and eager to pick a quarrel. There was a particularly bad one that Alan remembered concerning their neighbour, a Polish man, recently widowed, probably in his late forties. He and Alan's mother shared a love of gardening, especially growing vegetables; they would stand by the garden fence talking for what seemed like ages, swopping cigarettes and tips about fertilisers. Alan's father had accused his wife of 'carrying on' with this neighbour.

'Don't be ridiculous Tony. The poor man's wife has just died. He's lonely, just wants someone to talk to.'

The kitchen door slammed shut and shouting resumed behind it, so Alan went to find his box of bricks and dragged it into the sitting room. There was more shouting, mainly from his father and protests from his mother, then a definite loud slap. Alan stopped to listen but there was no more noise. Presently the kitchen door opened and his mother rushed upstairs, her footsteps sounding like the pretend machine-gun fire he and his friend made when shooting in the street.

Alan heard the back door slam and was glad his father had gone out.

They dropped the bombshell a few days later; he was to go away to school, the type of school where you sleep, eat and live. A boarding school. He could come home in the holidays.

'Your mother is going to stay with her friend Peggy for a while. At this school you will make lots of new friends. You know it will be a bit like that school Billy Bunter goes to, Greyfriars, is it? There will be midnight feasts and pillow fights, all jolly good fun.'

Both parents looked at him anxiously. He felt confused and didn't really understand what was actually going to happen. He certainly didn't know what to say. They must have taken his silence as acquiescence, as a few days later he was taken to a large department store and came home with two pairs of short grey trousers, a blazer, white shirts, a tie, pairs of grey socks, two grey woollen jumpers, vests and pants, a PE kit, a bulky overcoat and a stripy school cap. Alan was overwhelmed at the abundance of clothes that filled his bedroom and were a constant reminder of the imminent change about to happen. There seemed to be no going back.

A few days before he was due to go to the school he sat on the landing in the dark unable to sleep. His mother was in the sitting room sewing nametags onto all his clothes and he could hear the murmur of voices on the wireless. When the phone rang down in the hallway and his father came out to answer it, Alan stayed still and hugged his knees pushed against the banisters.

'Oh hallo there, Gerry, yes not too bad. Well, as far as I can tell, yes I think so, I hope so. Jean is still upset but what can I say? It all seems bloody unnatural to me. Yes, they worked together at the start of the war, land army, somewhere in Gloucestershire, not exactly sure where. I was in Egypt at the time. Who, Peggy? Yes, she's quite butch, you know, outdoor Amazon type, not unattractive, but really the whole business is quite messy, a bloody shock to the system. I just want to shield Alan. He's off to school at the weekend, better off out of it. Yes, will do. Cheerio.'

The phone slammed down. Alan was puzzled. Was Peggy a butcher, or an explorer? He knew the Amazon was a river. He hadn't heard his father swear before. He got colder sitting there so eventually crawled back into his bed and slept.

So that was the start of his new life, bundled off to school that weekend and apart from a bit of bed-wetting, he settled in fairly swiftly. Holidays were quiet affairs, spent either with his father, who had acquired a housekeeper, and moved to Shoreham, Kent, or with his mother and Peggy in their large bungalow near Reigate. It was only in his early teenage years that he began to think about the relationship between the two women. At school he had let slip he was going to spend the half term with 'Mummy and Peggy'. Questions about the identity of Peggy followed and Alan answered them in a matter-of-fact sort of way, not realising he was being lured into a trap.

'So are they lezzers then?'

This question came from a tall, white-faced boy who always looked bony, even with his blazer on.

Alan was confused. 'I don't know what you mean.'

'You know, women who fancy each other, like homos or poofs, but not men.'

Alan had no idea what they were talking about; he barely grasped the meaning of the word 'poof', and although there were 'nancy boys' at the school, apart from touching each other up he wasn't sure what else they did.

A fat boy called Roy tried to elaborate.

'Yeah, sometimes there's a butch one trying to look like a man and a normal looking lady one who acts like the butch one's wife.'

Alan remembered his father's phone conversation that he had overheard on the dark landing when the word 'butch' had been used.

He didn't understand at that stage the implications of these new words, and all he knew was that his mother had moved away and he had had to leave home to attend a boarding school. His parents had always argued, but since that summer's day when he had come in from the garden and seen Peggy sitting smoking at the kitchen table, things had gone from bad to worse. Her arrival had cast a shadow in his life and so he both feared her and blamed her. From that time the mention of her name set off a shudder of apprehension, felt even now over twenty years later.

Alan had reached the first of the riverside pubs he enjoyed drinking in but he didn't want to be inside just yet so carried on walking, the river to his left lapping over his thoughts.

SALLY

The kitchen at the house became her sanctuary. It was not really a comfortable room, more a place for cooking, eating or stoking the boiler. Its main attraction was warmth. Sally took to sitting in there every day after school, the kettle steaming peacefully on the stove. She would make some tea and sit on one of the mismatched chairs at the table, or the high stool next to the airing cupboard, and read *Middlemarch*. She found the slow gradual unfolding of the story soothing. She imagined the emptiness and space in the less populated lives of the characters as they walked through tall, draughty rooms or opened a door to a quiet street with only the sound of people or horses. From their windows she would see parkland or the arrival of a carriage on the drive. She escaped to a world of order, of servants polishing glasses and putting knives in drawers and arranging bottles of preserved fruits on shelves in the larder. It was a way of smoothing out the creases of the day, separating home life from work.

By contrast, the school she worked in was a modern, hard place with real problems that she had to deal with. The harshness was somehow confirmed by the geometric architecture of concrete and glass. The first-floor corridor was a rectangular circuit for badly behaved children on the move, endlessly chasing each other and only stopping momentarily when a teacher approached. The playgrounds outside were square arenas for bullying and fighting. Top storey windows had books or worse thrown out from a dangerous height to those underneath.

The discipline of some of her classes was not yet established. She must remember to take registers and follow up absences. She was not relaxed enough to be herself. One of the pupils had asked her why she never smiled, which had instantly made her grin but emphasised the constant tension she felt.

Her life seemed to be splitting into two halves. The chasm between her work life of unpredictable children and nerve-racking lessons contrasted greatly with her home-life, which was bound up completely in the house, surrounding heath, and village. As she crossed the threshold each day after work under the curve of the Georgian fanlight, she shut the door on the present. She took comfort from the kitchen, a warm meeting place, and the various people who gathered there. These people had become her friends and they would sometimes go for a pre-dinner drink at the pub on the corner by the pond. This was a new activity for Sally and it felt a grown up and sophisticated thing to do. The pub was populated with middle-aged men in striped suits who looked like journalists on the *Daily Telegraph*. Sally liked the little peanut machine on the bar that shot out a handful if you fed it 10p. At weekends, they would walk on the heath or wander across to Greenwich Park. Here Sally took childish pleasure in jumping the meridian line from the eastern to the western hemisphere. She was starting to belong in this part of London.

Shortly after Sally had moved in, Reg had given her a tour of the house. He had rented it since the mid 1930s with his wife Susan.

'Used to be nightingales on the heath, peaceful it was, there used to be cricket matches too in the summer, not so many cars then.'

Reg and Susan had always taken in lodgers and provided bed and breakfast for a variety of people. After the war, it was mainly businessmen. They would leave shortly after their eggs and bacon and return home fairly late in the evening. Now the house was a mix of students and teachers who, in Reg's mind, were much the same – a lot of reading and long holidays.

The tour had started in the kitchen outside the big pantry that was full of old bits of crockery, large cracked soup tureens and huge meat platters from some discarded dinner service. Reg informed Sally that Susan had collected various pieces from their day trips to Brighton where she would traipse around 'The Lanes' while he kept an eye on the gee-gees and waited in the pub. Sally imagined the two of them stepping out to catch the train and thought how well placed the house was for journeys to the Kent or Sussex coast. As the house took root in her imagination she saw a thread connecting it with Brighton and she briefly compared it with her own excursion with Jeff. Beyond the main kitchen was another pantry with a meat safe and two smaller rooms leading to the garden.

Reg continued the tour, climbing up the two flights of stairs to the first-floor landing with effort. He stopped on the landing, short of breath.

'Oh yes, we were here all through the war. We had a shelter down the end of the garden where the greenhouse is now, but we didn't always use it. We had an idiot staying here at the beginning, Harold Baker. Susan couldn't stand him. He would never come to the shelter in a raid, just sit there in that bath with a bloody saucepan on his head.'

They both peered in at an empty tub stained green around the taps, a damp flannel hanging over the edge. Pale sunlight shone through grime and frosted glass and a tin of Beatles talcum powder stood on the windowsill.

Reg himself lived on the ground floor. He had a large sitting room overlooking the heath with double doors that led through to a back room he used as a bedroom. An ugly metal-framed window had been put in shortly after the war, due to bomb damage. A bit of the Georgian building had disappeared and had been swept away with the rubble, a crude makeshift replacement slotted in to fill the hole. Concrete into brick.

There was only one room in the house that was not occupied, left empty with no particular purpose. It had been the old dining room with a hatch in the corner connected to the dumb waiter in the kitchen, still usable but no longer needed.

One evening when Sally had gone down to pay the rent, she could hear music as she knocked on the door. Reg shouted 'come in, ducks' and continued tapping his fingers on the arm of the chair with his eyes closed. 'Friday Night is Music Night' was his favourite radio programme and he didn't have a television.

A dark haired, middle-aged woman sat smoking in a chair opposite him and she nodded to Sally then turned away and stared into the fireplace. Although in the same room, both Reg and the woman seemed to be in their own worlds and oblivious to each other. Reg took Sally's rent then asked her to show the woman where she could make tea in the kitchen. Having waved her hands in the direction of the teapot and kettle, and taken Reg's particular tea caddy from the pantry, Sally was unsure whether she should stay or leave. The warmth of the kitchen decided her as the gas fire in her room only really warmed objects or people within six inches.

She and the woman exchanged pleasantries across the table and then fell silent. Sally asked the woman if she was in the area for any particular reason. The woman stared down at the table and didn't look up as she replied.

'I'm looking for my brother.'

'When did you last see him?

'The war, about 1942. I was just a kid.'

'You think he's in this area?'

'Maybe. I just heard he was living rough in south east London.'

The woman said nothing more but then embarked on a binge of tea drinking. She made one pot, put the tea cosy on, milk in the cups, placed the strainer, then spooned sugar into hers and stirred endlessly. After two cups, she seemed to wait several minutes or as long as she felt was decent, then the match was lighted beneath the kettle and the whole ritual started again. The tea making went on for over an hour. Sally was mesmerised by the constant drinking of watery tea, a challenge like a non-alcoholic beer competition. She had given up after the third round. No one knew who the woman was or where she came from or where she went. Reg's daughter came round the next morning to do a bit of cleaning and muttered something about a gypsy, tutting as she swept the floor. Reg had obviously given her a bed for the night to help out, and then she was gone.

PAMELA

Caroline called for me as usual. We told our mums we were going to the shops, which we always do anyway on a Saturday, so all we did was turn right at the end of our road instead of left. We met the girl with dark hair, who we now know is called Sharon, by the block of flats round the corner. They look like older flats than ours and there is a notice on a wall that says Peabody. I've seen it before and it makes me and Caroline laugh because we think of a green man with a pot belly. I noticed it again but didn't think I should mention it because Sharon might think we are babyish.

All she said was 'It's up two floors', not hallo or anything.

We followed her up the staircase. Maybe there are no lifts in these flats. Me and Caroline held our noses because it stunk of piss, but we did this behind her back so she couldn't see.

We got to a blue door, and there was a chair outside on the balcony but the door was bare, no number or knocker. The letterbox had a piece of carpet nailed across it, and Sharon knocked on it with her fist. Me and Caroline looked at each other. We had stopped holding our noses, and we felt a bit nervous because we didn't know what to expect. I looked at Sharon's bum and thought how her jeans looked good, nice and tight. My mum had bought me a pair from C and A but they were dark and stiff, and I didn't like them.

A man opened the door and Sharon stood back so that we could go in. Neither of them spoke but we got the message and went through into the hall where it was dark and stank of smoke. The man who had opened the door said 'In here girls,' and we followed him into what he called the studio. I don't really know what a studio looks like but this just looked like my nan's front room with the furniture taken out. There was a flowery wallpaper above the fireplace and someone had hung a white sheet on the wall opposite. In front of this stood a camera on three legs. Another man was looking into the camera and fiddling with it.

'OK girls, we are just gonna take some pictures of you, nice and quick and easy. All you got to do is take your clothes off over there, we'll go snap snap snap and Bob's yer uncle, Fanny's yer aunt.'

I didn't understand what he meant at first. I was nearly laughing at Bob and Fanny and I could see Caroline was thinking the same. The last thing we wanted was to get a fit of the giggles so we didn't look at each other. Just stood there.

Sharon said 'You need to take your clothes off so they can take photos. That's what you're here for.'

'You didn't say nothing about no clothes.' Caroline looked Sharon straight in the eye.

'Well, what did you think I meant? You ain't exactly Twiggy.'

'You just said photos. That's all you said.' Caroline was nearly shouting.

'I hope you haven't brought us no time wasters. We don't want no bleedin' kids wasting our time when we're all set up.'

The man fiddling with the camera spoke quietly. He didn't look at us, but his words made me nervous. I didn't feel like giggling.

Sharon turned to us both 'If you want paying you've gotta take yer clothes off. You don't get money for nothing.'

'I'm not doing it.' Caroline had that look in her eye.

The man with the camera looked up with a nasty face. I spoke before I knew it.

'I'll do it. I mean, it won't take long will it?'

Caroline looked at me as if I'd gone mad but she never was a dare devil. Like the time we said we'd jump off the pier into the river; we said 'one, two, three' and I hit the water with a cold painful slap but as I grabbed the ladder to climb out she was still standing there looking at me. I jumped. I didn't think or want to think, I just jumped into the unknown. Afterwards, I thought about how I had actually enjoyed that bit of time before I hit the water. I was in a space like a bubble for a split second before the smack of the water brought me back.

But this was different. It was not about being a daredevil. Now I was worried about what might happen if I didn't take my clothes off. That man might turn violent.

Caroline must have had the same thought and although she wasn't joining in she knew the man needed to know one of us was willing.

'I'll help you.'

I put my t-shirt and skirt onto the arm of a green settee in the corner. I was wearing a vest and I noticed my nipples were sticking out but I wasn't cold. I stood there in my knickers. It suddenly seemed difficult to take them off.

'And the rest.' Sharon spoke to the fireplace but I knew she meant me.

I don't know why, but I was shaking. I mean, it was just taking off clothes, something I did every day, but in front of strangers and the camera it was getting difficult. Caroline said quietly, 'come on, one, two, three.'

I suppose they took about 20 or 30 pictures. I just did what they said.

'Turn round a bit, that's right, put your hand on yer hips, look at the camera.'

It was over very quickly. I was still nervous as I put my t-shirt on back to front, and rammed my feet into my plimsolls. The man with the camera spoke to me and Caroline, looking at us for the first time.

'This money we're giving you is for modelling. Now it didn't take long. All you had to do was stand there with no clothes on. Nothing happened, it was all done professional like. This money means you don't tell no one, not your parents, not your friends, no one. If we find out you've told anyone there will be trouble, big trouble, and people could come to harm. Remember, don't tell no one.'

As we left the room, the man who had let us in gave me a £5 note. It was screwed up tightly and I gave it to Caroline who put it in her sparkly purse. We left on our own. Sharon didn't come with us.

Once outside we ran up the street, faster and faster, until we reached the shops. We stopped, out of breath, and astonished at what had just happened. We stood by the bus stop just looking at each other. Slowly things got back to normal. It was Saturday, it wasn't raining, people were out and about with their kids and no one knew.

'Let's buy some sweets, loads of them.'

'Yeah, loads of them.'

'Then we can go into town and spend the rest.'

Caroline turned and looked at me. 'Yeah, but Pam, you've gotta buy stuff for you, not me. You were the one who did it. I bottled out.'

'Yeah, well you ain't no bleedin' Twiggy.'

We laughed for ages, or at least until the bus came.

ALAN

Alan stood behind the till in his shop sorting through a box of small prints that were all muddled up after a busy Saturday. He automatically looked up when he heard the bell. At first, he didn't recognise the young woman as the light was behind her. She smiled as she put a package on the counter.

'Hallo, I've brought some more prints.'

Alan knew he recognised her but couldn't think from where. He looked blank.

'I saw some of the prints I had painted in here last week so thought I would bring them directly to you this time rather than the other place.'

She untied the package and Alan realised what she was talking about. Ten pages from a book on the 'Victorian River' slid onto the counter. The Thames barges now had brown sails against pale grey clouds, and the prison hulks at Woolwich were washed with a murky rust and black.

'Ah yes, I see. The thing is, Rob and Alison deal with the artists and I just sell the prints in here.'

'Yes, I know. I don't like dealing with Rob. He makes me feel a bit self-conscious. I like Alison, but she's not always there.'

Alan couldn't help but smile at hearing that someone was resistant to Rob's charms.

'I think I know you from somewhere.'

'Yes, we met at the local history library, the gallery. You liked my landscape painting, you said it was "expressive". I sold it, there was a red dot.'

He remembered her now, of course he did, her shiny brown hair, curly and short, her quick smile and dark eyes.

Before he had time to think, Alan had blurted out 'Would you like to have a drink? We could go to one of the pubs along the river. There's a good one just beyond The Trafalgar. In fact, it's shown in one of the prints you brought in. Look, here it is.'

She leaned forward and peered at the tiny image, where a scratchy pair of bow windows was just visible at the water's edge behind a large sailing ship. She wasn't wearing perfume but he could smell a faint fragrance, maybe shampoo or soap?

Smiling, she lifted her head and looked at him.

'Yes, that would be nice. When do you finish work?'

It had been that easy. He couldn't quite believe she had said yes to his clumsy invitation, but half an hour later she was waiting by the Cutty Sark, studying the wooden figurehead that faced out to the river, the carved hair forever forced back by the wind.

He had time to look at her as he walked across the vast space that housed the old sailing ship, the tea clipper in dry dock. From this distance, Marie, (he had remembered to ask her name before she had left the shop) did not look like the kind of girl to agree to have a drink with him. Her denim dungarees and Monkey Boots made him feel a bit like an uncle or awkward teacher in his conventional jacket and grey trousers. Was this suggestion to have a drink a mistake?

It wasn't a mistake. They found so much to talk about – painting, old buildings, living in south east London. It seemed they found a subject, any subject, and immediately they were off, thoughts spilling out endlessly. Two hours after meeting by the Cutty Sark they both decided they were a bit hungry so went into the nearest café without even looking at the menu. Two and a half hours later, as they parted, Alan put a hand on Marie's shoulder and looked into her eyes.

'I really enjoyed this evening. I mean really enjoyed it.'

'Me too. I'm looking forward to next weekend.'

They had arranged to see an exhibition the following Sunday.

He didn't kiss her. They just smiled at each other before she went into her flat. Alan walked home, his head spinning with conversation. He was oblivious of the tramps congregating for the night outside the doss house and avoided the drunks outside the pub halfway up the hill. He finally came to the wide expanse of the heath where he breathed deeply and was full of optimism.

The following morning, after he had lifted his bike out of the shed and carried it up the steps and onto the heath, he sat on the wall and waited for Rob. The third station on the old Crystal Palace line was a short ride away.

As soon as Rob arrived, they took off. A fast and furious ten minutes later, they stopped in front of a single storey hut standing at right angles to the main road. Rob was irritable and breathless, having been reminded that Alison's bike had no gears.

'This isn't that interesting. Just a scabby old scout hut.'

'Yes, it's all that's left of Lewisham Road Station, just the ticket office.'

They crossed the road, which was quiet and empty on this Sunday morning. Alan looked over the bridge and along the track in the direction they had just come from. He had an old photo from the local history library of the same view taken in 1903. There were far fewer trees and no tall buildings, just glimpses of a scattering of roofs. The photo had been hand tinted by someone who had made it look more like Italy than Lewisham. Two Edwardian women on the platform wore dresses of lemon and pink, and the roofs were painted an unlikely terracotta.

He thought of Marie.

Rob offered Alan a cigarette and they stood staring down at the track. They then crossed to the other side where you could see two or three bridges disappearing in the distance like a perspective drawing. These would be running under the wide avenues of Brockley, with its grand Victorian villas and names like Tressilian, Breakspears and Wickham.

'So where were you last evening? I phoned at about 6.30 to see if you fancied a drink.'

'Actually, at that time I was already having a drink, at a pub on the river, with a girl, lady, woman. Anyway, she's called Marie.'

Rob turned to face him with his eyebrows raised as he blew smoke from the side of his mouth.

'You're a dark horse. Is this girl, lady, woman, anyone I know?'

'Yes, she's one of the art students who paints the prints from your cut-up books.'

'Oh, that Marie, pretty enough in a rustic sort of way, a comely figure, rosy cheeks, looks like something from an updated Thomas Hardy novel, "Tess of the dungarees". But I wouldn't have thought she was your type.'

'What is my type?'

'Skirts, necklaces, heels sort of thing.'

'Like Fiona you mean?'

'Well, yes I suppose so. She's the only type I have to go on.'

It didn't take long to reach the site of the next station, Brockley Lane. They turned up Wickham Road, a broad avenue of large old houses mostly split into flats. The width of the road and trees felt relaxing after the main road and they cycled two abreast.

There was not much to photograph at Brockley Lane. They found the entrance to the station, boxed in by hoardings, and now a second-hand furniture business. What had been the station master's house stood on the opposite side of the road and the track itself still ran over their heads and was carried across the road by a traditional bridge. There were some bricked-up arches that may have been part of the station, and some closed public toilets, but not really much evidence at all. The current Brockley station was the other side of a bridge crossing the railway line going north to south. Given its use and importance it seemed strangely out of the way compared with the site of the long-closed Brockley Lane.

'Will you see her again, Marie?'

'Yes, she's invited me to a party next Saturday. She lives on that estate in Deptford, you know the one, full of students and social workers. I've asked her to come with me to an exhibition on Sunday. We'll have to postpone Nunhead until two Sundays time if that's all right with you?'

'Suits me. I could do with a proper lie in.'

SALLY

'Right, quiet please, listen everyone. Yes, you too, you the boy on the end.

I want you to imagine you are a photographer in a park. Give me the name of a park someone, yes you, Linda, OK, Dulwich Park. Give me another somebody. Yes, Douglas, Brockwell Park. And another, yes, Norwood. OK, so you all have a park that you know that you're familiar with. So imagine that you are in that park with a camera and you're taking photos of a friend. Maybe they are posing for you, pretending to be a fashion model or someone famous like a footballer. You are messing about having fun, taking lots of shots, different angles. You are in a secluded spot, lonely, no other people about. You are surrounded by bushes and trees and hidden from the rest of the park. You take two maybe three films, then the light changes. It's getting darker so you decide to go home. You have enough shots for one day.'

Sally then asked the class to gather round a board where she pinned up a large photo of a model posing for a fashion shot by some shrubs in a park.

'So that evening you develop the films in your own darkroom at home. You've chosen the best shots from your contact sheet and you print three or four. Then you decide to enlarge one of your prints, like this one here on the board, so your friend is now huge and you see more of the background. You notice some detail in the bushes behind your friend and you're not certain what it is. So you go back into the darkroom and blow it up to get a closer view.'

Sally replaced the photo on the board. This second one showed the model much closer from the shoulder to the knee and moved to the left of the image.

'Can anyone see what that is behind the model on the right in the bush?'

'Could be a dog Miss.'

'Or a ghost.'

'Yes, it could be either of those things but you're not sure. Are your eyes playing tricks? So you carry on enlarging just that part of the photo.'

Sally put a third photo on the board, this time with the model gone and the focus entirely on the bush.

Zooming in to this extent made the object more obvious, though still blurry.

'It's definitely not a dog.'

'It looks like a person.'

'That's a face and an arm held up.'

The whole class seemed to lean forward in an effort to see. Sally continued.

'The next day you see on television that a person has been found murdered in the park where you took the photos. Have you somehow captured the murderer in a part of your photo? Or was the victim hiding in the bushes shortly before they were killed? The day after that you arrive home and discover your house ransacked, the photos are gone and the negatives too.'

The whole class was silent and attentive and watched Sally as she moved towards the paper and charcoal.

'So was it the murderer in the bushes then, Miss?' asked Stephen.

'I don't know, it could have been.'

'Which park was this, Miss?'

'What I have just described to you is a film, and it was made in a park quite near to here.'

'So, it's not true, it never happened?' Nick looked across to Sally.

'I told you, it's a film, a story.'

Nick was insistent. 'But was it based on a real murder?'

'I don't know.'

Sally addressed the whole class and explained what she wanted them to do. She asked Sharon to give everyone three sheets of paper and Roy to give out the charcoal.

It seemed to work and was one of the best lessons she had had with that class. They were absorbed in their drawing and forgot to be disruptive or noisy. This was the fourth-year class that Sally had had such trouble with at the beginning, that had been so hostile and loud. Now she was just getting to know them, certain characters stayed in her mind. Neil, the fat blond boy who looked out at the world through suspicious squinty eyes but had a dry sense of humour; Kofi, who had long elegant fingers and produced feathery expressive drawings; Sharon the girl with black hair who looked as though she wanted a fight with someone, anyone, but drew with exquisite detail in pen and ink. Then there was Sharon's friend Nick who always sat with her and expected other pupils to move up and make a space for him if he was late. Richard and Karl had calmed down a bit since the cut finger incident, though Sally always felt a sense of menace around them, and neither ever appeared to be totally involved in a lesson. They seemed alert to noises outside in the corridor, their thoughts elsewhere, planning some meeting for the next break. They came to school to attend lessons because they had to, but the far more important reason was to see their friends, threaten their enemies, and set up deals that would spread and flood into their streets outside.

As Sally walked around the room speaking quietly to individual pupils, a strange calm had fallen that may have been related to the afternoon sun which had gradually crept round the building and was now streaming through the windows. The art room was on the top floor of a rectangular block that faced a large inner space open to the sky. The ground was concreted over and not used. On the opposite side, Sally could see the science rooms, rows of Bunsen burners glowing at slightly different heights.

'Miss, the sun's in my eyes. I can't see properly.'

Neil, the fat blond boy put his hand across his face. Sally said nothing, but silently lowered the blind and silence was restored, the only sounds being the scrape of charcoal and the occasional sigh or cough.

Sally flicked through her register, checking she had taken it today. She noticed Nick had missed the last five of the Tuesday lessons, a row of fat noughts in among the herringbone of diagonal lines, like holes made by dropped stitches in a piece of knitting. As the lesson ended and the class filed out, Sally stopped Nick and asked about the absences.

'It's OK Miss, my tutor knows. It's an arrangement.'

She would need to speak to his tutor, Mr Gibson, and find out what the explanation was for all these absences.

Sally locked the classroom and walked down the corridor thinking of Nick. The strong late afternoon sun showed all the scratches and scrapes on the floor ahead and became worse on the staircase where more feet would have trodden.

She wasn't keen to talk to Mr Gibson. He was a smarmy man with dark hair and a bulgy cushion of a stomach under which his trousers were tightly belted as if oblivious of the bulk above.

His office door was open and he looked up over his glasses at Sally's tentative knock.

'Could I have a quick word?'

He moved a heap of files and directed Sally to sit on the empty chair. He then offered her a Polo and, when she refused, took one for himself. It looked like a mini lifebelt on his tongue.

'Nick, unusual character, yes his absences are known about and accounted for. Last term he was sent to a reform school so he wasn't here at all. This was before your time. In September he had a fresh start here but was required to see a probation officer weekly until half term. I assume that day in the week was when he missed your lesson.'

He turned over a piece of paper.

'Tuesday.'

'Yes.'

Mr Gibson held the piece of paper in mid-air uncertainly.

'Why was he sent to reform school?'

'Some incident with another boy, an accident maybe, some tomfoolery that got out of hand. You know what boys are.'

She didn't, and said nothing, waiting for further explanation.

It wasn't forthcoming and Mr Gibson put the piece of paper on top of many others. He seemed anxious about something as he then moved it onto the filing cabinet behind him and placed a heavy glass ashtray on top of it.

There was an awkward silence, and Sally wasn't sure if this was the end of the interview or just a pause.

Mr Gibson seemed to return his focus to Sally and her reason for being there. 'So, you see, Nick was telling the truth; he did have an official reason for missing your lessons.'

He leaned forward, rested his hands on the desk and attempted a genial smile, which did not fool Sally. The man was still agitated about something, and preoccupied. He concluded the interview by standing up and saying, 'So there you have it, all above board.'

Sally walked back down to the staffroom. The corridors were calm and empty now that most of the children had gone home. She grabbed her coat and went out through a side entrance. It felt good in the fresh air. She put her school bag on her shoulder and walked towards the bus stop.

The discussion with Mr Gibson felt inconclusive. Surely children were only sent to reform school if something serious had happened? What had he meant by 'tomfoolery'? Mr Gibson had appeared rather uneasy and, having spoken to him, she didn't feel particularly reassured about Nick. There didn't seem to be anything else she could do.

STANLEY

He just wanted to sit down, rest his head on the thin cushion, and close his eyes. Yes, that was better, a bit better. He felt slightly dizzy and couldn't remember the last time he had eaten. Was it three days ago or more? He had lost track.

Lost track of many things, the days of the week, where he had hidden his money, where his tins of food were kept. There wasn't much water left in his plastic container but he couldn't remember where he got it from, and even if he could he doubted he would have the energy to fetch it. Could the boy help him? Would the boy come again? So, he just sat still, sometimes focusing on the smeared brown window panes but there was nothing to see. He couldn't work out if the lack of clarity was due to his failing eyesight or the dirt.

He was aware of the passing of the day by the changing light. It could be a pale lemon in the morning on one side of the caravan and a gradual shifting to a more golden light on the other side, which he vaguely understood was evening. Some days it was just different tones of grey. The nights were dark and confusing and he slept in short snatches.

Sitting there, he could sometimes hear the buses loud and clear, pulling up to the bus stop, their engines throbbing, then pulling away. Some days he even heard the ring of the bell, ting, ting, as the conductor gave the all clear to the driver. Or people, shouting, kids maybe, the sounds ebbing and flowing like the tide, clear then faint. The most troubling noise was the barking, which seemed close, then distant, but it was pretty constant. Nothing he could do about it. Just sit tight.

VALERIE

Valerie Jones, Pamela Webb's housemistress, strode across the car park, her thin blonde hair flapping. She carried a white plastic bag of books and a navy leather handbag swung over her shoulder. Pushing the door to the school open forcefully and not troubling to slow down, she shouted across to the receptionist who had just arrived. 'Morning Mary, lovely day.'

As she reached her office, she stopped momentarily to put the key into the lock and flung open the door increasing the size of the chip in the bright red paintwork as it swung back and hit the filing cabinet.

The chip caught Arthur Simmons's eye, followed closely by Mrs Jones's mini skirt as he loomed into the doorway, filling it like a blockage.

'Oh, Mr Simmons, you startled me. Did you want something?

Arthur Simmons swallowed then swallowed again as he tried to eradicate what he might want from Mrs Jones in his secret thoughts. He edged further into the room, uncertain but furtive.

'The fact is…' He stood awkwardly.

Mrs Jones grabbed the white plastic bag of books from the chair,

'Sorry, it's so cramped in here. Sit down Mr Simmons.'

He arranged himself in the chair, adjusting his position several times as if how he actually sat would assist what he had to say, and he cleared his throat twice.

Mrs Jones appeared to tidy her desk to hide her unease. In the ten years she had been at the school she had only ever spoken a few words to Mr Simmons, ranging from 'Good morning' to 'Please clear up a mess in C4. Someone has been sick.'

The longest conversation had been an embarrassment to both of them and had taken place in the staffroom, which was more neutral territory, and had the added comfort of other people sitting nearby. On that occasion, Mr Simmons had been similarly ill at ease as he informed her that she needed to talk to the girls in her house about 'soiled matter' being wedged behind the pipes in the toilets.

'I assume you are talking about sanitary towels, Mr Simmons.'

'Yes,' he hissed. 'There are incinerators in the girls' toilets, all functioning. All the lazy cows have got to do is use them.'

'Of course, I quite agree. It's outrageous. I'm sorry you have to deal with such a disgusting task. I will talk to the girls in house assembly tomorrow. Thank you for telling me, Mr Simmons, and I hope we can put a stop to this type of thing immediately.'

Now here he was again, sitting in her office, so early in the morning. He had obviously been waiting for her to arrive, and it seemed as if all their conversations were destined to be about difficult and unpleasant matters.

Arthur Simmons was overcoming a number of hurdles in his mind: talking about something important to a young woman; talking to a woman who was apparently superior in her job, certainly paid more; and talking to a woman wearing a mini skirt. He would have preferred to have dealt with Miss Lloyd but she was busy all day and her secretary had referred him to Mrs Jones in the first instance. He felt more at ease with Miss Lloyd; she was older, almost granny age, with sensible covering clothes and just a glimmer of a long-vanished sexuality, enough to make him feel manly but not threatened. She was friendly but distant in terms of class, age, education – so many things. He liked how he thought Miss Lloyd might think of him, as physically strong, a decent bloke maybe a bit rough round the edges but capable of keeping all the caretakers and cleaners shipshape. He felt respected as someone who could be trusted to keep the building secure, and he knew she understood the breadth of his knowledge of all the rooms, cupboards and outbuildings. She understood the weight of his responsibility, measured by the number of keys attached to his belt.

He was less certain of Mrs Jones. He wasn't sure how he appeared in her eyes. Somewhere between a necessary nuisance and an uneducated yob? No, that was probably too strong. She must value the job he did, appreciate that it wasn't always easy, since she knew some of the unpleasant facts as she had to discipline the girls.

He could tell from her accent, somewhere northern, that she wasn't posh, and the way she moved was slightly clumsy. She made him feel awkward. She was too young, too female, and wore skirts that were too short. The other caretakers joked about her thighs, and her body was a hot topic of conversation in their office. All the young female teachers were fair game, some of the pupils too. It was all quite natural, just red-blooded blokes, no harm in it.

So, here he was in her small office with a difficult piece of information. At least she was sitting down behind her desk and his view was of a light-blue shirt and a small creamy necklace. Her shoulder-length fair hair was pushed back and she looked at him from under a straight-cut fringe.

'Well, Mr Simmons. What's this all about?'

He had planned what to say and roughly in what order. He had even scribbled a few notes on the back of an envelope, but now it just came out as a jumble. In the end, it was the only way he could do it. Her hard northern accent made him defensive. It never occurred to him that she might be equally nervous.

'The thing is, in our office we have calendars, photos, you know pinned up, nothing too strong, of you know pin ups, girls in bikinis and such like, page three type of stuff. Usually they're on the inside of our lockers but we do bring in photos to put up on the board.'

Some of the images on the board swam into his mind along with Mrs Jones's legs, and threatened to confuse what he had to say, so he swallowed and looked down at the desk in an effort to concentrate. Similarly, Valerie Jones wondered where this topic of conversation was leading, and felt a prickly heat under her collar. She kept silent.

'The photos are just normal, nothing too mucky.' He had meant to say 'explicit', had looked it up in a dictionary in the library, but in his haste and embarrassment had forgotten it. 'We all bring stuff in, some more than others. It's just a bit of fun, you know a laugh. Well, last Thursday one of the lads came in with some new photos, and we was all having a look when St…, I mean one of the other lads, said he recognised the girl in a couple of the pictures. Once he said it we all knew what he meant. I mean, her picture's been on the telly so much recently there's no mistaking. It's Pamela Webb. It's her all right. The lad who brought the photos in wanted to take them home and pretend it hadn't happened. He thought he might get in trouble, but I persuaded him it could be important. So I said I had to tell someone but wouldn't give his name, so on that basis he gave them to me and I have them here in my pocket.'

He patted his chest and paused for breath. Valerie Jones realised she was required to speak.

'Well, ah, yes thank you for telling me Mr Simmons. I, erm, think your information could be important.'

She was torn. Should she ask to see the photos of Pamela to verify her identity in case this could be wasting police time, or should she refer him directly to the police in the form of Detective Inspector Wilson? She felt hot and claustrophobic in this small office, shut in with Mr Simmons and his nasty photos.

She had to ask one question.

'The photos you think are of Pamela Webb. Are they naked shots?

'Yes, they are.'

The phrase 'child pornography' was swirling round her brain but she didn't want to say those words to Mr Simmons; she didn't really want to say anything more to him. The implications of his information were horrible in so many ways. The poor girl was only eleven. She couldn't bring herself to ask to see the photos. Somehow she would feel defiled just by looking; she wasn't up to it now, but maybe later. This was too confusing, she had never had to deal with anything like this and was unsure of the procedure. Her overriding thought was to end this conversation and get Mr Simmons out of her office. His physical presence and the early morning heat from the radiator was oppressive. She stood up.

'Yes, Mr Simmons, I think it's best if you see DI Wilson as soon as he arrives, which should be,' she glanced at her watch, 'in about 20 minutes. Meanwhile, I'm sure we both have a lot to do. Thank you for bringing me this information. As you say, it could be important.'

She said the last sentence with her hand on the door handle to let Mr Simmons out. He nodded and left the room with his shoulders and fists clenched, the rectangle of photos just visible in the chest pocket of his overalls.

Valerie Jones locked her office and walked rapidly towards the staffroom, which was empty. She made for the sink behind the serving counter where two large urns stood steaming quietly, and ran her hands under the cold tap. She splashed her face twice, lifting her fringe, and looked into the small mirror. She needed time to process the information Mr Simmons had just given her. Who on earth would be interested in photos of naked eleven-year-old girls? It was beyond her understanding and well beyond her experience. She filled a mug and drank gulps of water. Valerie Jones then did something she rarely did these days; she sat down in the staffroom, taking a seat by the window, and stared out at the trees.

Her parents' voices came into her head. They had been fearful of her coming to teach in London ten years ago.

'They'll be difficult kids, lots of immigrants. Why not find a job here? Plenty of schools in Nottingham,' was her mum's comment.

'You'll need yer wits about you,' was her dad's contribution.

She had started as a geography teacher but had particularly enjoyed being a tutor and had gradually taken more work in this area and after three years applied to be deputy head of house. Four years after that the old head of house retired and Valerie was her successor. Her mother was puzzled at this promotion.

'Surely, you'll be wanting children of your own Valerie. You can't leave it too late.'

Valerie wasn't sure she wanted children, and Graham, whom she had married straight out of college, was similarly uncertain.

'No rush, is there?' he said, although they had been married eleven years.

'Valerie does things differently,' was the explanation her mother arrived at for most of her actions. She had started doing things differently by passing the eleven-plus, then choosing to stay on for A-levels in the sixth form, then growing to 5ft 10in tall while her brother was only 5ft 8in, for wanting to play football and having to make do with hockey, for taking geography at university and finally deciding to move to London. The only thing she had done that they fully understood was to marry Graham, and this was as a result of pressure.

'You can't go to London on your own. You can't live in sin. He's a decent lad with a proper job, and you could do far worse.'

Yes, it could have been far worse but it could also have been far better. Their marriage had got stuck at a sort of middling set of shared habits, where they hardly spoke but just got on with working, eating and sleeping.

The door to the staffroom opened and Miss Lloyd crossed the room.

'Good morning, Valerie, I've just seen Mr Simmons. Could you come to my office. I think we need to talk rather urgently.'

As the two women left the staffroom, Arthur Simmons took his place on the chair outside the room used by the police. He sat and waited with his important information, sifting through his bunch of keys.

SALLY

She had a huge canvas bag filled with empty shoe boxes collected from various shops in the precinct. During the course of a week she carried them all to school on the bus. At times, it was squashed and difficult but most people manoeuvred round them and ignored her. By Friday she had enough for a whole class to make pinhole cameras.

Sally actually looked forward to some of her lessons and the class of first years were a chirpy bunch. They were noisy and at times too enthusiastic, but did respond to her instructions and genuinely seemed to enjoy whatever project was set. Mr Gibson had asked her how she was getting on with this particular class. He said he 'had his eye on them', as various other teachers had complained about the behaviour of some of the boys. Sally said the behaviour was generally good and she enjoyed teaching them. Mr Gibson had then become ingratiating, remarking 'Well, you obviously have them under your spell' and 'Some teachers just don't have the discipline like you do.' Sally found all this embarrassing and never quite knew how to respond. She was still perplexed about the meeting concerning Nick. She did not feel that Mr Gibson's explanation had been adequate. He had seemed distracted as if he was withholding something. After every meeting with him she felt irritated.

She told her first-year class about the pinhole cameras and they were incredulous.

'You are joking, Miss.'

'You mean we can take photos without a camera?'

'No, but seriously, Miss, you must be having us on.'

But they all put on the old shirts and aprons, laid the newspaper out across the tables and prepared the paint.

Sally moved the plastic water pots away from the edges of the tables and gave them all a small paintbrush and their own shoebox. After telling them first to write their name on the underneath she asked them to paint the inside of the shoebox very carefully with black. They would need two layers. The intention was that every child would take at least four images with their pinhole camera. At first Sally thought the photos should be just taken in the classroom but the pupils persuaded her otherwise. She decided to ask some of the sixth-formers to help her out. If they could escort the younger children in small groups, it would give them a broader choice of environment for the figure they were photographing.

The sixth-form lessons were also ones she enjoyed. The absence of discipline problems and the group of interested and motivated students was a refreshing contrast to the rest of the week. Discussions of drawing techniques, development of themes and possible next steps to higher education gave the work an intensity and focus. There were twelve students in her A-level drawing class, seven girls and five boys. A few weeks after the beginning of term, an American boy joined the school as his father had work in London and moved the family from Boston. From the start, he seemed much older than his English counterparts and several of the girls obviously fancied him, admired his accent, his dress sense, but most of all his confidence. He would address Sally as an equal, which she found a little disconcerting. In fact, the one drawback with teaching the sixth form in general was that Sally felt too close to them all in age. She shared their taste in music and was only four or five years older than them. So although she felt authoritative in terms of teaching and subject knowledge, she was unprepared in life experience. This was not always a problem, but sometimes she was made aware of it, and on those occasions it undermined her general approach to these students, making her tentative and a little uncertain.

There was nothing tentative about the American boy whose name was Jim. He would stroll into the classroom early as Sally was cutting paper or cleaning brushes.

'Ah, mý favourite lesson with my favourite teacher.'

At first the other sixth-formers would raise their eyebrows at Jim's audacity. They were too self-conscious to address a teacher in that way having been brought up with a sense of subtle deference that Jim lacked. But because of his relaxed manner they soon accepted him as an interesting addition to their group, and increasingly included him in conversation and social invitations.

Sally had to admit she enjoyed talking to him about his life in America and his travels. His family were renting for a year in London and it transpired that their house was very close to Sally's new home on the heath. She said nothing about where she lived, just enthusiastically agreed that it was a lovely area. Jim used the word 'lovely' a lot and he pronounced it in a half-mocking Shakespearian English manner. It was obviously not a word he had used before and he seemed to have acquired it as part of his new life in Blackheath. And, like drinking tea with milk, it was not something he would continue to do once he returned to America.

Meanwhile, he used it to describe his parents' new house, the garden, and the amusing small car his father drove. He also used it to describe Sally, or Miss Parry as he refused to call her, though only to himself, not to her face. Even he was not that bold.

The pinhole cameras were in general a success with the lively first-year class. Some of the photos were blank as the pupils had opened their pinholes too soon or for too long, but enough of them were recognisable images. Sally laid them all out at the start of the lesson and the children crowded round to get a good look.

'That's Michael by the tree.'

'Janet looks all blurry.'

'Why is mine all blank?'

They talked about exposure times that had been noted in their books and then stuck their own photos next to the figures. Sally kept copies of all their photos for a display, and once they had left the class, sorted through to look at the best ones. One girl had been particularly keen and taken great care to achieve some clear results; in a class of twenty-eight there were about ten good images. Sally put them all away in a drawer to deal with later and made her way to the staffroom.

Andy, the history teacher, was standing by the coffee machine counting out change in his hand. He looked up smiling at Sally's entrance.

'Ah, the very person. Do you have 10p? I'm desperate for a cup of coffee.'

He looked straight at her but she couldn't meet his eyes; just his presence made her nervous. It was as if she was fourteen again and had a crush on one of the sixth-form boys at her old school. The fact that his opinion of her was increasingly important made her quite self-conscious. All fingers and thumbs, she searched for her purse and handed him the coin then started blurting out information about the pinhole-camera project. This was a desperate attempt to make conversation and it was the first thing that came into her head. But he seemed genuinely interested.

'Yes, I saw a couple of boys taking photos by the gates. I thought I should question them because you know recent events, the missing girl and everything. They seemed to know exactly what they were doing and were taking it very seriously. Not bad for a class with a reputation for discipline problems.'

'Yes, Mr Gibson keeps telling me about their reputation. They were in small groups and did have sixth-formers with them.'

Sally was quite distracted by his physical presence as he sat down opposite her in a chunky knitted jumper, his hands resting on the knees of slim, black jeans. Everything about this man was attractive – his easy smile, his sharply cut slightly spiky hair and the soft Scottish accent.

'Have you been there?'

Although she was only half listening, Sally was dimly aware that Andy had been talking about the Crystal Palace and the prehistoric monsters. She focused fully on the conversation again.

'No, I've heard about them but never actually visited the park. Just seen the edge of it when I get off the bus.'

Andy went on to describe the interior of the Crystal Palace in its heyday and colourful images whirled around in Sally's mind like a Victorian kaleidoscope.

'It was a giant glasshouse of an unimaginable scale, nearly two thousand foot long and four hundred foot wide, where a stuffed elephant would appear the size of a toy. Ornamental ponds, a fountain of crystal and a row of palm trees ran the length of the building. They were flanked with statues, Roman figures, sphinxes, tall pillars covered in coloured hieroglyphics and beautiful objects from all over the world, made from rosewood, ivory and teak. Can you imagine the light flooding into such a vast glass space? Or the sound of raindrops pattering on the roof?'

'It sounds incredible. I hadn't realised it was so huge.'

'Yes, and that was just the inside. We had our sports day last summer on the running track that was once a football pitch. Some of the boys were impressed when I told them the FA Cup Final was played there for twenty years at the beginning of the century, though some of them obviously didn't believe me. The gardens stretched all the way down the hill, Italian terraces, cascading waterfalls, bandstands.'

'Oh yes, I remember reading that D.H. Lawrence came to musical concerts at the Palace while he was living nearby and teaching in Croydon. I thought of him as I stepped off the bus on my first day and wondered if I would hate teaching as much as he did.'

'And do you?'

'Too early to say.'

'Anyway, apart from a few pieces of statues and some crumbling steps the prehistoric monsters are the only things left. There is a boating lake where they can still be seen lurking on islands in the undergrowth.'

'The Palace burned down didn't it? Do they know what started the fire?'

'Not really. Some say a cigarette end fell through the floorboards and set fire to the rubbish underneath, but no one is certain.'

'When was this? Was it before the war?

'Yes, 1936.'

'I remember my dad saying he could see the glow in the sky from his bedroom window as a kid. That would have been over thirty miles away.'

'Well, it's still an interesting place. Well worth a visit.'

Andy stood up and reached for his leather jacket on the back of the chair. Sally waited for him to say something like 'Are you free this Sunday? I could show you round.'

He seemed to hesitate and looked at her for a few seconds as if he understood what she was thinking. It was then his turn to seem embarrassed and he turned away, saying nothing.

Sally stood up quickly, feeling awkward. 'Well I must go and clear up.'

Andy looked at her again. 'Thanks for the coffee. See you later.'

Sally had finished tidying her art room. The paintbrushes stood in a pot of hot water, the tables were wiped and the drying rack was emptied. She took the pinhole camera photos out of a drawer and laid them out on a table to select several for display. She had to smile at some of the poses; there was Leroy flexing his arm muscles, Angela pouting like a model and Derek with his tongue stuck out. It was difficult to recognise all of the children in such blurry circumstances. One girl, (Sally checked the register and was reminded of her name, Jennifer) who had seemed really keen and determined to get the exposure time right, had taken three clear images. Jennifer was a bit of a loner in class and had teamed up with a quiet withdrawn boy so he appeared in the first image, hunched up and slightly scowling. The next photo showed him closer and slightly smiling. Sally had never seen him smile before and here was evidence of a different child, possibly as he might be at home – away from the noisy, pushing corridors of the school. She imagined him stroking a rabbit in the corner of some quiet garden. Sally sighed at the difficulty of getting to know so many children in such a large class and how the quiet frightened ones could so easily be neglected at the expense of the noisy demanding pupils. In the third photo, he was completely out of focus and turning away, but this time the background was clearer and Sally recognised the dark-haired girl in her fourth-year class. Yes, it was definitely Sharon, but she was standing on the wrong side of the gate, out in the street, holding what looked very much like a cigarette. Evidently she was not where she should have been, in her lesson, but why would she leave the school and then hang around outside where she could so obviously be seen? Sally decided to ignore this scrap of information. Any investigation of it might involve Mr Gibson, and she didn't feel like talking to him about anything. Also it felt a bit like snooping. She decided to think about it, maybe talk to another teacher, possibly Miss Lloyd, but not Mr Gibson.

ALAN

You could hear the party from the next block. Alan and Marie climbed the stairs and stood outside the open door from where the music blared. They pushed their way into the hall, carrying the two bottles of beer that were the passport to any party. The thin passage was lined with people smoking various sizes of cigarette. Alan had borrowed a donkey jacket from Rob as he didn't want to feel conspicuous in this arty set. They reached the kitchen and hovered around a table full of half empty bottles. As Alan reached for a handful of crisps he realised too late that someone had emptied beer all over them and he stood there with a soggy handful, unsure where to put them.

Two women and a man sat on the floor by the sink. They looked like a row of exotic collapsed birds. One woman wore shiny turquoise, the other lemon silk and the man was all in black with heavy eyeliner. The woman in lemon silk ran her tongue around the outside of her lips like the small hand of a clock. The man in black licked her shoulder while the woman in turquoise rubbed something squidgy on her arm, which Alan realised was a piece of raw liver. He was genuinely fascinated, but Marie pulled his arm, muttering something the only word of which he could make out was 'pretentious' before she pushed him back out into the hallway and into another room. Given the squashed crowds in the rest of the flat, this was strangely empty, both of furniture and people. Two huge speakers throbbing with reggae stood by the far wall and a mattress was rolled up against another. One of Marie's friends grabbed her and they started to try to talk against the booming music.

Alan sat down on the fireplace and, feeling he should attempt to join the party, took a couple of swigs from a bottle of he knew not what. It turned out to be some sort of sweet strong spirit and it immediately filled his body with a glow, so he had some more.

A black man with a huge afro stumbled into the room holding the hand of a white woman with lank blonde hair. They started dancing half-heartedly.

Alan smiled. He was enjoying himself watching all these people. He looked across to Marie, who had taken off her fur coat and was wearing a wine-red dress with a tight waist and a full skirt. Her dark curly hair was tied back with a piece of fabric, her forehead was white, her eyes brown and her lips plum. Seeing her like this, across the room at a strange party, confirmed his attraction for her; the plump (although she would have hated the word) body, the smiling face and her general sense of eagerness. She exuded warmth and friendliness and, most extraordinary of all, she was with him. He must have been smiling again as the man with the afro leaned across, grinning widely and holding something that looked like a burning roll of paper.

'Good shit man.'

'Yeah.' Alan smiled and nodded companionably until he realised the man was offering it to him.

The effects of the sweet drink relaxed him enough to think 'yeah, why not' and his brain said 'you can just pretend to inhale'. He put the slightly damp paper to his lips and before his brain's advice had time to reach him, he had breathed in deeply. Whoosh, his head felt as if it had gone up the chimney behind him and exploded above the roofs of the London flats. On the second drag he closed his eyes smiling to himself at the strength of the sensation and wondering how long the swirling in his head would last. The swirling made him think of the nearby river, the ebb and flow of the water. He imagined himself being swept along by the current. He opened his eyes and spoke to the man next to him, 'Is the tide coming in or going out?'

'Far out, man.'

They both snorted with laughter at the appropriateness of the clichéd response. The man took the burning roll from him, stood up slowly and tottered towards the door. The girl with the lanky blonde hair was still dancing in the middle of the room.

She swayed independently of the music, completely disregarding the rhythm, a sort of lurching from side to side on the spot, like a skater who has reached the end of the ice. Her velvet smock looked grubby, and she seemed oblivious to the room or any of the people in it. Alan watched and started imagining which artist might have liked to paint her. He came up with a few possibilities, but settled on Hogarth. It suited her look of rawness, a pinched face against the cold, lips like shrimps. Why did she look so vacant, so removed from the room and the party, dancing in a distracted and pained way? Had she escaped the suburbs? He imagined her life in a mock-Tudor semi in Bromley, a thin bed, carefully made, in a teenage bedroom, childhood flowery wallpaper at odds with black posters of heavy metal guitarists in leather trousers. Was she an art student too or just someone who lived in the flats?

'You don't have to try so hard,' Alan wanted to tell her, but she was far away in some chemical haze.

Someone sat down next to him in the fireplace. It was Marie, and she squeezed his arm.

'Are you all right? I mean you don't know anybody here.'

'I'm fine. I'm worried about that girl there. Do you know her?

'Never seen her before.'

'She looks unhappy, slightly desperate.'

She pulled him to his feet.

'Come on, dance with me.'

The following morning, Alan and Marie walked across the bridge towards the gallery. The river was grey and lumpy and the only boats were the barges carrying rubbish or the occasional river police.

The warmth inside was a welcome contrast to the windy bridge. Marie removed her beret and loosened her scarf as they walked through into the first room. She spent some time studying each painting. Alan was familiar with most of them but still enjoyed seeing the originals. He sat on a bench in the centre where he had a good view of all the paintings and could pick out his favourites. Marie crossed the room and sat next to him.

'I like the fact that they are of London, you know, some of the places I recognise, but they are a bit too literal for my taste. Of their time, I suppose. My mum would like them.

Alan hesitated. He didn't know if Marie was putting him in that parental category and was sensitive to the fact he was older than her by seven years. Did she think of him as some old romantic bourgeois?

He was particularly interested in showing Marie the Pissarros and ushered her into the next room.

'Look, here's Crystal Palace. You can stand there and look at almost the same view today. Well, obviously the Palace has gone and there's a petrol station but the direction and the width of the road are the same.'

'Oh yeah, that's where the buses wait at the end there.'

'And this one here.'

Alan strode towards the next painting and, despite herself, Marie found his enthusiasm infectious. He wanted to tell her about the exact locations and see if she recognised where they were. He was so keen to explain and she began to be interested because she knew the area and had actually lived near one of the painting locations in her second year at art college.

'And this is the one that has intrigued me for a long time, ever since I first saw it at university. It's one of the reasons I'm researching the old Greenwich to Crystal Palace railway.'

Alan stopped in front of a painting that had a steam train running through the centre. The land was a green slope and there was a scattering of Victorian villas in the background. Marie thought it was rather dull.

'It definitely has the wrong title.'

'What do you mean "the wrong title"?'

'Look, it says "Penge Station" but underneath in brackets "this is probably a view of the station now known as Penge West" which suggests an uncertainty.'

'Well, a lot can change in,' Marie squinted at the date, 'just over a hundred years.'

'There's something wrong here about the lie of the land. Those two slopes are not in Penge, but where are they?'

'Lie of the land indeed.' Marie smiled up at him.

Alan did not acknowledge her quip and was still preoccupied with his explanation. 'You see he, Pissarro that is, had only been in London for a short while, under a year in fact, escaping the Franco-Prussian war, so he can't have known where he was half the time. He would have been stumbling about sketching, not knowing where Sydenham started and Norwood ended. I mean, I was at school there but I'm not sure either.'

'And I'm a foreigner too, escaping the Midlands, so I don't have a clue.'

Marie sat on a bench and looked towards the grey light of the river. Alan joined her and they both considered the painting from a distance.

After a few minutes, Alan broke the silence.

'So, if it's not Penge Station, where is it?'

Marie turned to look at him.

'How many stations on that old line have you visited so far?'

'Four.'

'How many left?'

'Five.'

'So there is a strong possibility it might be one of them.'

'Maybe.'

A week later Alan and Rob stood outside the gates at Nunhead Cemetery. It was sharp, cold and blustery. Most of the leaves had fallen weeks ago, but any stragglers would be finally whipped off the branches today. The sun appeared sporadically. There hadn't been much to photograph at Nunhead railway station. It had been rebuilt in the 1920s in a slightly different position from the original station and was a single storey, nondescript building. Alan had noticed a poster for a missing schoolgirl stuck to one of the pillars by the entrance. The photo stayed in his mind, as for some reason he connected it to his mother. There was a similarity to an old black and white image of her as a child. It was something to do with the expression on the girl's face and the Alice band in her hair. Alan took a few shots for the record and suggested visiting the cemetery as they were so close. It would feel less like a wasted visit after the disappointment of the station.

The gates to the cemetery were set back from the road. Looking through them you could see a long straight path flanked by tall trees that led up an incline to a Gothic looking folly, or possibly a chapel. It was a dilapidated building with two pointed spires and a dark gaping doorway. It could have been a scene introducing a 'Hammer horror film' or an episode of *Sherlock Holmes*. He could picture a Victorian hearse waiting outside, the horses shaking their heads, irritated by black plumage, men in dark stovepipe hats and ladies in stiff liquorice jackets adorned with Whitby jet.

'Well and truly locked.' Rob shook the gates, more in irritation than with any hope of budging them.

'I'm sure we can get in somewhere,' said Alan, leaning his bike against the wall and noticing the upturned torches on the gate posts. He'd read somewhere in a book on London cemeteries that they represented 'life extinguished' and the sight of them made him shudder.

'I bet kids are in and out of here all the time.'

It was a kid who showed them the way in. He appeared from one of the old low houses opposite the cemetery gates with a small mongrel on the end of a lead. They followed him the length of the high wall and turned up a cobbled path past an old urinal with a green ironwork canopy. The boy and his dog disappeared, then reappeared a few minutes later. The boy beckoned 'In ere'.

They found themselves by a thick hedge with a low gap at the bottom.

'Bloody hell,' grumbled Rob.

The path under the hedge came out into a partial clearing of birch trees where random gravestones stood at various angles of collapse; what had once been an ordered row, part of a plan, was in the process of being rearranged by tree roots, pushed from underneath, covered by creeping growth on the surface and hemmed in by trees above – a sort of three-dimensional takeover. There was a thick quietness.

Alan took photos of broken statues, their faces stained with bird lime as he stumbled over chunks of stone, cracked and broken, the dates of birth and death a numerical jigsaw. Celtic crosses were covered in lichen and crumbling columns had stone ivy encircling upwards, long overtaken by living green ivy. Layers of fake and real. He came across a sleeping angel lying the full length of a grave, looking so peaceful and comfortable, her hair spread on a stone pillow and wings resting.

Alan thought of Marie. She would love this place and he wanted to bring her here, to share it with her. He was sure she would be more enthusiastic than Rob whose interest in the whole project was waning with the colder weather. Marie had become interested in his old railway project and had bought a large sketchbook to record all the visits. He hadn't wanted to leave her on Sunday evening. His flat had felt cold and empty on his return.

Pushing through a tangle of shrubs, he came to a straight path and realised it led down to the locked gates at the bottom. He saw Rob sitting on a grave, his legs apart, and between them two stone arms reached out, holding each other, a sort of united in death pose.

'Don't move Rob, I just want to take a shot, between your legs actually, the two arms clasped. It looks good, very good.'

Rob looked down.

'Christ, I hadn't realised, how macabre, reaching out from the grave, to each other. Have you finished yet, David Bailey?'

He stood up and lit a cigarette, rather clumsily, as he hadn't removed his leather gloves.

'My feet are numb.'

'Yeah, let's go. Now all we've got to do is find our way out of here.'

They looked down the path towards the shut gates where the row of old houses stood and beyond them layers of London. Alan knew they were looking directly towards the city but no landmarks were visible on this grey day. The layers stretched ahead, stacked up like different scenes in a theatre, ageing, fading and disappearing or altered, repainted and rebuilt, but constantly changing.

November

STANLEY

He was so cold, he hadn't moved all day, apart from first light when he had managed to reach his 'commode', a bucket under the sink. That had made him dizzy. The journey of a few feet had taken him how long? Ten minutes, half an hour? He couldn't tell.

When the whole operation was over he slumped back onto the heap of blankets, all smelling of dog and covered in hairs. Why was that? He pulled the eiderdown up over his head like an old woman wearing a shawl. It was still cold, his eyelids were heavy, his whole body exhausted, and he felt as if he was drifting into sleep. Then the pain of the cold nudged him awake, and he tried to move his hands into his pockets, looking for cigarettes. He didn't find any, but there right at the bottom was his lighter. He slid it up his leg and out into his hand. He gripped it tightly and rested for a moment, breathing slowly, holding it close to his chest, running his fingers over the smooth metal. He could hear a dog barking; sometimes it was loud then it would appear muffled but it was a consistent noise. Why was a dog barking? Who did it belong to?

The paraffin stove was just across from his pile of blankets. He couldn't remember using it, but he must have done last winter, or was it last week? Whenever it was, he felt confident there would still be enough paraffin to give some warmth. The thought spurred him on as he leaned forward, the eiderdown slipping from his shoulders, but he couldn't reach it. The paraffin stove stood sturdily on its three metal legs a few feet from him next to a bench seat piled high with old newspapers. He sank to his knees and was level with the little window where the flame would appear if he could only get his lighter to work. He made every effort to press down his thumb, but it was no good; he couldn't push hard enough. He closed his eyes and rested, then had another go. He pushed hard, and again, and again, then suddenly there was a flicker of flame. With renewed energy he almost fell onto the stove and connected the flame to the paraffin wick. There was a whoosh, and as he realised it had worked he fell back among the heap of blankets, relieved. The lighter dropped to the floor, forgotten, where it fell, still lit, onto a patch of spilled paraffin. Sitting back feeling the warmth, his eyes closed, he didn't notice the second whoosh. A faint smile of achievement crossed his face as the eiderdown slipped to the floor. The effort had exhausted him but now there was heat, quite a lot of heat, and smoke. There wasn't usually smoke like this. Half-opening his eyes he saw the flames run along the dirty scrap of carpet, saw them leap up the pile of newspapers and tickle the hem of the grubby curtains.

Oh no, oh no, he groaned. He was exhausted physically but also now emotionally at the thought of what was happening and how he lacked the strength to do anything about it. The smoke was making it difficult to breathe and his eyes were streaming. He coughed feebly and made an attempt to stand but his legs were too wobbly. As he sank back again breathing was becoming impossible, and he was surrounded by grey swirls of smoke. He could see no more than a few inches in front of him. He felt weak, unable to act. The crackle of flames and the clouds of smoke were swallowing him, and he couldn't see anything now.

He was confused. His mind played tricks on him these days, jumping around in time, jumbling up the order of things. He was back in another fire, a blaze of forty years ago.

He had never seen anything like it.

Where was Muriel?

He had lost her in the jostling crowds. The fire engines were coming from all over London but even if they sent every engine in England he doubted they could save the Palace now. Puny jets of water were arching into the flames and making no difference whatsoever. He was pushed one way then another, part of a heaving mass, all come to see the Crystal Palace, the landmark for miles around, burning down. People were crowded onto nearby rooftops, had climbed trees, cars, anything to get a better view.

He had even seen a few small planes circling from a distance. The Croydon Aerodrome must be doing a roaring trade. A woman next to him was openly sobbing onto the sleeve of a stranger. Where was Muriel? Had she managed to get to the edge of all these people and make her way home?

A huge roar erupted from the crowd as the south transept fell, metal twisting and glass melting, pouring down like golden syrup. He could feel the heat stronger now. He was squashed and couldn't move, wedged in on all sides by a heaving mass of bodies.

He'd never seen anything like it.

The heat was unbearable. He spluttered ineffectually, his lungs taking in small clouds of smoke and tried to breathe out into a bigger smoke swirl that now filled the confined space. The small caravan had become an incinerator, its tiny metal windows jammed shut

Then a searing heat took hold of his foot as the flames caught his trouser leg, followed by a pain that was sharp, intense, but not as bad as the smell of what he dimly realised was his burning flesh.

Minutes later a woman in one of the nearby prefabs ran up to the telephone box on the parade and dialled 999. As she put the phone down, the caravan exploded, the door and windows flew through the air, allowing the freed flames to lap up the oxygen and leap high into the night sky.

IRIS

A small group of teachers and pupils stood waiting outside the school. It was a grey day, overcast and still, with not a breath of wind. Valerie Jones was talking intently to a small girl in a pale blue anorak with a fur-lined hood carrying a pink, plastic rucksack. Caroline, Pamela Webb's friend, had been persuaded to take part in a reconstruction.

A net curtain in one of the large houses opposite the school was pulled back slightly so that Iris could get a better view. She cleaned in this house for Mrs Lewis two days a week and was familiar with the school as she also cleaned there for the other three days. Switching off her vacuum cleaner she stood by the window watching Caroline. Iris knew what was going on, although she didn't quite understand the point of it. It seemed highly unlikely that any of the same people who had been present when the girl disappeared would be around today. It was a quiet road, wide and leafy, the large houses occupied by professional people, people who were busy, out at work or lunching or shopping. These professional people didn't have time to sit staring out of their windows and if they did it was more likely they would sit at the back and look at their gardens where it was more peaceful. Such people would have a choice of rooms to sit in, which lessened their chance of having seen anything.

Ray Wilson, with a mounting sense of irritation, was dealing with photographers from the local newspapers. They were getting in the way, making the little girl more nervous than necessary, and adding to the mounting hysteria. Miss Lloyd clutched a silk scarf around her neck and appeared tense and anxious.

'Detective Inspector, I think we should start quite soon if we want to avoid break time and I think I most definitely do want to avoid that.'

Valerie Jones had her hands on Caroline's shoulders and she could feel the poor kid shaking.

Wilson walked over to where they stood. 'Now, Caroline, we're ready to start. Are you clear about what you have to do?'

'Yes, sir. I have to walk across the road to the bus stop, then back to the school and cross to the side gate. Then you'll walk with me to the sweet shop and back to school.'

'Good girl. Now don't worry about any of these photographers. Just remember, we want to do everything to find your friend Pamela and this could help. You're doing a very important and brave thing.'

Caroline bit her lower lip, gripped her rucksack and set off.

Iris wondered why they had sent the little girl dressed up as Pamela Webb towards the shops. How did they know she hadn't gone the other way towards the roundabout?

Iris smiled as Mr Johnson from next door seemed to be having a problem getting his Jag out of the drive, which was blocked by a group of photographers and their cameras. There had been resentment ever since the old maternity home had been knocked down in the mid-1950s and the school had been constructed on the site. Residents said it had spoiled the tranquillity of the road and it continued to be a source of annoyance in such a wealthy area. There was the minor disruption every morning and evening when hordes of children swarmed to and from school. Parents' cars clogged the roads, children shouted or swore, there were scuffles, litter was thrown into the gardens and crisp packets blew around like autumn leaves.

Iris lit a cigarette and sat by the broad windowsill watching the police and photographers below. The girl had temporarily disappeared but was obviously expected to return, as everyone appeared to be waiting.

She thought the people in this road got off lightly. They should try living in her block of flats, then they would understand what trouble meant: kids starting fires in the rubbish chutes and taking the light bulbs on the stairwells, making them even more dark and threatening when she staggered home with the groceries. Most people preferred not to use the lifts, which smelled of urine or were liable to break down. Only last week she had nearly fallen over a couple of kids. They were standing in a corner on the second flight, snogging, and she had started to apologise but the boy had sworn at her so she hastily made her escape to the next flight where the light was still working.

The coloured kids were something else, like a tribe apart, with their funny hair, standing on street corners in threatening groups. Her son Neil had a friend called Wallace whose parents were from Jamaica, and he had come home a few times. Her husband was not keen on this friendship but Iris liked Wallace and tried to make him welcome. He and Neil did their homework together and as far as she could see he was a good influence.

It was the older ones who scared her, the men who wore tea cosies on their heads and made strange clicking noises when she passed them on the balconies. One of the pubs near her flat had been taken over by these men who played dominoes in the public bar. They would slam the pieces hard down on the table with much force and noise, shouting and jumping up with excitement. Iris thought this was quite entertaining but her husband decided they wouldn't drink there any more.

The people in this road were cushioned by money, and noisy children twice a day were a minor inconvenience. There were the weekends and the holidays when they could pretend the school did not exist. From the window, the cleaner could see her own pale blue Ford Capri parked on the drive. She enjoyed coming here to clean, and could imagine for two days a week that she actually lived here in this soft-carpeted, bees-waxed furniture, gleaming-mirrored, house. Her employer, Mrs Lewis, was pleasant enough, but fortunately never at home so Iris could drift from room to room having imaginary conversations.

'Hallo, darling, did you have a good day at work? Oh really, shall I get you a drink? Whisky?' Her husband in this fantasy life alternated between looking like Paul Newman and Robert Redford. She would iron his shirts in the bleached clean kitchen, smelling the steam of the fresh linen blown dry in the generous garden. It was very different from ironing at home, her rickety ironing board squashed next to her cooker, the washing smelling vaguely of fried food. Driving to this job was an important part of the fantasy. It established she was a car owner and set her life on the first rung of the possibility of living in such a house. Coming on the bus would have spoiled everything.

She picked up the ashtray to empty it and saw that the girl had returned with the man she took to be a policeman. Would this enactment help anything? Probably not, but at least it showed willing. She felt sorry for the mother of the missing girl, not knowing, just waiting, and she could only imagine the horror of that situation. But despite sympathising with the mother, she wasn't able to share her small piece of information. She didn't feel able to talk to the police. Iris needed her cleaning job at the school; her family depended on it and they couldn't exist on Mrs Lewis's money alone. Iris opened the window slightly to let out the smell of smoke then quietly closed the door and went down the beige carpeted stairs to the kitchen.

Wilson ushered Caroline through the main school entrance just as the bell rang for morning break and children tumbled out into the playground. The photographers threw their cigarette ends into the gutter or ground them under the heels of their shoes and drove away. Caroline was visibly relieved and her shoulders relaxed as she removed the pink rucksack and blue anorak. Valerie Jones picked up the fraudulent possessions and smiled at the girl.

'Well done, Caroline, that can't have been easy. Are you OK?'

Caroline nodded and seemed anxious to return to her lessons and pick up the normality of a school day.

Valerie Jones walked back to her office wondering at the effectiveness of such a re-enactment. She doubted anything would come of it. In the absence of any new evidence, the newspapers wanted to feed the public and remind them that something was being done. The girl had been missing now for several weeks and still there were no leads. As she sat at her desk, Valerie saw through the small glass window in her office door Mr Simmons walk past with one of the cleaners. It reminded her of the last time she had spoken to him and of the photos he had in his overall pocket. She needed to speak to Ray Wilson and find out the significance, if any, of them. Looking at the notepad on her desk of things to be achieved that day she wondered when she would find the time.

SALLY

Sally had heard the word 'delicatessen' but had never actually been inside one. There had been no such shop in the comfortable but dull suburb where she had grown up. Now, living in this fashionable area of London, she enjoyed exploring the rich variety of shops every weekend. So one Saturday she walked to the top of the village, past the bank, the launderette, and into 'Friedrichs'.

In the delicatessen, two elderly women with grey plaits wound around their heads (like a human version of one of their loaves of bread), wrapped unusual cheeses or slices of pâté studded with dark red cherries in waxed paper. The shop was full of food Sally had not seen before: curved sausages, dishes of pickled vegetables, dark chocolate-covered biscuits dusted with icing sugar. There was a variety of bread, shiny loaves black as treacle, spirally rolls covered in seeds, walnut sticks and round white loaves sprinkled with sugar. Sally just enjoyed standing in the shop, taking in all the unusual food and interesting smells. It was so busy that no one seemed to mind that she didn't buy anything. She would go back another time. Maybe she could invite some friends round for a meal and surprise them with sophisticated food.

Later that afternoon, Sally was ironing some clothes in the kitchen. This was not something she did often as it involved plugging the iron into a light bulb socket that hung over the table. Even to Sally's non-scientific brain this seemed dangerous, but there was no other choice. She had a small transistor radio by her side and was listening to a rather melodramatic play. She dimly heard someone shouting her name, then the door opened and Claire stuck her head in.

'Sally, I've been calling! There's a young man at the front door asking for you.'

Sally put the iron down and turned the radio off, frowning. Who could it be?

'He's quite dishy, if you ask me.' Claire disappeared back up the stairs.

As Sally left the warmth of the kitchen and climbed the stairs to the hall she saw Jim, the American boy from school, standing in the doorway. Her first thought was, how the hell does he know where I live, but she ushered him in quickly to keep out the cold of the gaping door.

'Jim, I'm just down in the kitchen, this way.'

Normally Sally would take friends up to her room but that was far too intimate for this situation. She felt awkward and unsure. Was it usual for sixth-formers to visit their teacher? It was not something she would ever have dreamed of doing herself. She remembered an invitation from a history teacher for a small group of her own sixth-form to go round for a drink after their exams. It was a stiff, restrained gathering with the teacher offering them small glasses of Sherry for the girls and half-pints of lager for the boys. This experience flitted across her brain as she asked Jim if he would like some tea.

'Actually, Sally, I've brought some good Moroccan and that Doors LP we spoke about. Do you have anything to play music on here?'

Good God, thought Sally, what am I meant to do? This doesn't feel right.

'I don't smoke. We can't smoke that here.'

Jim looked around and Sally thought the room must seem like a museum to his eyes as they took in the iron plugged at the light bulb with its old-fashioned plaited flex. She followed his gaze across to the fireplace with the meat platters arranged on the shelf above and then to the greasy red gas cookers and the wooden draining boards of the butler sinks.

'This is cute. It's what I love about this country – so much history just hanging around in people's homes. Can we play music?'

Sally explained that she only had a record player in her room and hoped the implication was clear, that they wouldn't go up there. Jim accepted the offer of tea and sat on a chair, smiling at her.

'I guess I've surprised you calling round.'

'You could say that. How did you know where I live?'

Jim explained he often walked his dog on the heath as a way of getting to know the area. One evening after school he'd seen Sally from a distance walking up to and then disappearing inside the house. He sat back in his chair, looking very relaxed and Sally wondered if he had already sampled the 'good Moroccan'.

'I often come up here with the dog. It's such a good place for her to run around. You get this fantastic

360-degree view, like standing in a saucer circled by houses with that dome of sky overhead. I love it.'

He continued talking, saying how much he liked London, particularly green places like the heath and Greenwich Park. It seemed he didn't know many people his own age and Sally understood that he was lonely. In fact, she started to feel sorry for him but she also still felt awkward at the situation. Jim asked her if she ever went to hear the Sunday lunchtime jazz at the Greenwich Theatre. Sally nodded and said she did sometimes.

'I go with my old man. He's really into jazz. Last week he played a few numbers on his trumpet as a 'guest American'. That really made his day. Eat your heart out Miles Davis! Hey, a piano.'

Jim stood up abruptly. He had just spotted Reg's pride and joy standing in the far corner near the window. It was a beautiful piece of Arts and Crafts furniture and had a small candleholder at each side. Jim sat on the stool.

'OK if I play?'

He started by thumping out a fairly competent 'Lady Madonna' then progressed to a more jazzy piece before a medley of 1950s musicals. On the chorus of 'Oklahoma', Reg shuffled into the kitchen, beaming, and sat on a chair next to the fireplace tapping his walking stick on the floor. Claire also came in, obviously curious about Sally's visitor. She stood by the piano smiling at Jim. As he finished playing with a theatrical flourish, they all applauded.

'Not bad. You can come again young man.'

Reg stood up and went to put the kettle on.

Sally stood on the doorstep at Jim's departure. She would not feel entirely relaxed until he was out of the house. In other circumstances she would have welcomed his friendship, even encouraged it. Jim turned to say goodbye and asked her if she would like to meet him at the Sunday jazz the following day. Once again her emotions got the better of her and she was tongue-tied and embarrassed, unable to speak clearly or easily.

'It's not possible. I just can't.' She knew she was blushing and Jim's calm just added to her sense of agitation.

'Anyhow, take this.' He handed her the LP. 'You can give it back at school.'

'Thank you, Jim.'

Sally closed the door.

BRENDA

Pamela's mother stood at the bus stop feeling cold. There was no one else waiting and the timetable had been torn away, leaving a rectangle of rust. She already had doubts about this expedition and hanging about was not helping. Five minutes later the bus arrived and she was on her way. There was no going back.

Brenda Webb had made an appointment to see a clairvoyant in Catford and had the address written on a scrap of paper in her pocket. Since Pamela had disappeared, she had become almost housebound, desperate to stay near her recently installed phone. Her days followed a strict routine: get up, wash and dress, have a cup of tea and a cigarette. She would then walk down to the police station to check on any new developments and return home via the shops for a newspaper and any bits of food. Friends called occasionally, and her mother brought round a casserole or fish and chips. The friends tried to encourage her out.

'Come to the flicks with us, Bren. It will take your mind off things.'

But Brenda did not want to take her mind off things for one second. She needed to be alert and available, near the phone, ready for any information, good or bad. This not knowing was like a constant dull ache throughout her body. She felt as if her life was on hold and her body in a permanent state of tension.

She had been recommended the clairvoyant by one of her mother's friends whose husband had recently passed away.

'It was eerie what she could tell me about Jim. I mean, I'd never met the woman before.'

So maybe she could find out something about Pamela. Brenda felt that by visiting the clairvoyant she would at least be doing something. And you never knew, it could lead somewhere, provide a few clues.

It was a difficult house to find. The streets of old houses all looked the same to Brenda who was not familiar with this area. The theme of street names was trees and it wasn't until she had almost reached the end of Beech Avenue that Brenda spotted Ash Walk. It was a cul-de-sac, blocked at the end by a railway bridge, and had an unvisited air about it. She re-read the crumpled piece of paper in her pocket even though she knew the number by heart, and rang the bell.

The door was opened by a woman with a wrinkly neck and strongly dyed black hair. Brenda stepped into the hallway, which was dark and smelled of cats. In fact, the whole house seemed to have layers of smells, as if they had piled up over the years and no one had ever opened a window. Faint whiffs of cooking were overlaid by washed clothes and floor polish, then more cooking smells. None of these had completely escaped and seemed to be stuck in corners. Brenda was ushered into a dingy front room with heavy velvet curtains pulled across most of the window.

'Sit down, dear. Of course I know why you've come. So sorry for your trouble.'

The woman too was a layer of fainter smells. Under the Eau de Cologne Brenda detected slightly unwashed clothes and a dusty talcum powder. They had spoken on the phone a few days ago and Brenda had been asked to bring something that belonged to Pamela. She pulled a blue plastic hairbrush out of her handbag, a few hairs still lodged in the spikes. They sat opposite each other at a small round table covered with a green chenille cloth on which Brenda placed the hairbrush. The clairvoyant reached across and held both Brenda's hands. Closing her eyes, she muttered several times, 'You must be strong, you must be strong for your daughter.'

Brenda found this unnerving and didn't like the look of the clairvoyant's hands that were sprinkled with brown spots. She was relieved when her own hands were replaced gently on the table and the woman picked up Pamela's hairbrush, holding it tightly and breathing deeply, her eyes still closed.

'Pamela, your daughter Pamela, she is a good girl. She is calm and sensible.'

Still clutching the hairbrush, she continued.

'I see water. She is separated from you by water. I think she has crossed water to be where she is now.'

'Water?' Brenda frowned.

'I think she's safe. I think she's with someone you know.'

Brenda fidgeted as she felt a cat brush up against her leg under the table. It made a faint purring sound, and as its tail flicked against her knees, she shuddered.

Had this all been a mistake? The dark-haired woman was giving her the creeps; she hated cats at the best of times and there were at least two of them slinking about under the table, brushing against her in the dark. Brenda was starting to wish she hadn't come when the woman, still with closed eyes, asked her, 'Do you know anyone in Northern Ireland?'

Brenda was taken aback and answered with a dry mouth. 'Maybe, I'm not sure.'

'Well, there could be a connection.'

This one question was the only point of interest to Brenda. The woman continued in a very general way, saying that Brenda was a good mother and that she should not give up hope. She said she was starting to get a stronger sense of Pamela and that Brenda should return next week as she may have more to tell her. Brenda had already decided the whole thing was a bit of a con and was impatient to leave. After about half an hour she stood up and put on her coat. The dark-haired woman smiled as she took the money and said she hoped to see Brenda again. At the front door, she said something else about Pamela as a parting shot. Brenda thought this was a last-ditch attempt to get her to come for a second reading and so disregarded it as she hurried out into the street.

She retraced her steps to the bus stop, trying to get rid of the feeling of revulsion at the prowling cats brushing against her. It was the sense of cats being hidden under the table and not being able to see them that had disturbed her.

As the bus crawled through the south London traffic, she mulled over what the clairvoyant had said. She had never really discussed Pamela's father with anyone except her own mother when she discovered she was pregnant. He had been a soldier in the army and she had met him with a group of friends in the pub. They had gone dancing a few times but generally the pub, the Bell, was their meeting place. It was on one of these evenings after a few drinks that she told him she might be pregnant. He hadn't appeared too concerned but a week later told her he was being posted to Northern Ireland. The last time she had seen him was at Gypsy Hill station, where they had stood on the platform waiting for his train. He had said he would phone. She never heard from him again.

Two days later, Brenda sat opposite Detective Inspector Wilson in his office at the police station. She had come, as requested, to report back on her visit to the clairvoyant. This gave her a small sense of purpose and she had taken more care with her appearance. A smudge of pink lipstick matched two plastic earrings. Wilson was required to type up the general gist of her visit and send it to the local newspaper. After establishing a few facts, he tried not to sound impatient with his questioning.

'Did the clairvoyant say anything you considered useful?'

'Well, she asked if I knew anyone in Northern Ireland. I've never told anyone but that's where Pamela's father might be. He was in the army when we got together. I don't know if he chose to go there or was posted, but when I told him I was in the family way he said he had to go to Northern Ireland pretty sharpish. I thought he would be back after a few months, at least some kind of leave, but I never saw him again. Never heard nothing neither. He might be dead. Who knows? It looks pretty scary out there when you see stuff on the news.'

'So, he did know you were pregnant?'

'Yeah, I'd told him the week before that I thought I was, then that night at the Bell I told him it was definite.'

'Was he pleased at this news?'

'Kind of, well, I thought he was because he ordered extra drinks. At the time I took this to be a celebration of my news, but thinking back I was wrong. He just liked a drink. Any excuse would do.'

'And you have had no contact with Pamela's father since then?'

'None. Last time I saw him was at the station. We said goodbye on the platform, he said he would phone, then got on the train. That was it. I never heard nothing. He didn't even know if I had the baby or that it was a girl.'

Wilson shifted in his chair.

'Did the clairvoyant say anything else you thought might be worth following up?'

'She said Pamela was across the water. She thought she was safe and with someone I knew.'

'I suppose across the water could be a river, like north of the Thames, or even a lake.'

'I took it she meant the sea, but I don't know.'

Brenda then started telling Wilson about the cats under the table and how the whole experience had given her the creeps. She described the room and the woman and the smell of the house and said she didn't want to go back there if she could help it.

'OK, thank you.'

Wilson shut his notebook, thinking he'd heard enough of this nonsense and he had plenty of other things to do.

Brenda stood up and pushed her chair noisily under the table. She stopped at the door and turned back to Wilson.

'Oh yeah, the last thing she said to me just as I was leaving, outside in her hallway, she said, "There is a smell of coal somehow connected with Pamela."'

Wilson omitted this last bit of information in his report. In fact, he'd got the whole piece down to just a few lines. Still, in the absence of any hard facts, it kept the public informed and the newspapers happy, but in his opinion it really was a load of old cobblers.

ALAN

Marie and Alan stopped at the T-junction. The road behind them had been following the route of the old railway track. It would have had to cross this main road here but there was no sign of a bridge. They looked straight ahead, arms resting on handlebars. It was not difficult to see where the station had been. A large square block of modern flats stood on the corner. There must have been a bridge that took the track across the road and then onto the Crystal Palace.

This new arrangement for visiting the stations on the old railway suited them. As Marie was usually at Alan's flat on a Sunday morning, it made sense for her to accompany him. It gave Rob the option of staying in bed on a Sunday (it also gave him a geographical option as to where the bed was as he didn't have to rush back to meet Alan). It suited Alan as it meant he spent more time with Marie and it suited Marie as she was becoming genuinely more interested in the whole project.

'That's the site of the station.'

'Hard to imagine and even harder to imagine a bridge crossing the road here.'

'Maybe the road wasn't so wide then.'

Alan took out an old picture of the station and passed it to Marie who held it stiffly with her black woolly gloves. The photo showed a station building with an old black car parked on a slope leading up to the ticket office. A squat van with two oval windows in the back that looked like eyes was parked directly under the sign 'Southern Railway, HONOR OAK STATION'. At least it suggested there had been people about. Most of the photos of the stations on this track were empty, probably taken once the line was closed, just before the track was taken up and the buildings demolished.

'I wonder who that funny van belonged to. It could be the station master. I bet he brewed his tea in that room there, and then came out through that door and across to the ticket office.'

The black woolly finger stabbed at the photo. Alan looked up.

'Shall we walk along a bit? According to this old map there was quite a substantial coal yard behind this station. Then there should be a row of houses and shops, hopefully still there. Let's lock our bikes to these railings.'

Marie linked her arm through Alan's.

'I'm so glad I came today. Lucky for me that Rob had to go away this weekend. I hope he's away next week as well.'

'To tell you the truth, I think he was missing having a lie-in on Sundays and now with the cold weather he seems less keen on these visits.'

'Good. I'd like to come next Sunday. Is that a cemetery?'

Grey trees stood in clumps behind a waist-high wall, beyond which Alan and Marie could just make out a few gravestones in the long damp grass. They walked past several shops and a post office, the cemetery still on their right, until they reached a crossroads with a hotel on the corner.

'Alan, I'm going to buy some sweets. There's a shop we just passed further back. You can take photos or something. Why don't you go into the cemetery and sit on one of those benches? See you in a minute, OK? Won't be long.'

She was off like a child in the playground.

Alan crossed the road to take photos from a distance. The position of the hotel building was starting to make sense in relation to the vanished railway station. He could imagine passengers arriving late in the evening and needing somewhere to stay, and he could hear the station master giving instructions: 'Yes, sir, there is a hotel about a hundred yards away. Just turn left at the bottom of the slope. Thank you very much, sir, mind how you go.'

Without the station, the hotel looked a bit lost. Despite a grand entrance porch, it appeared run-down and not much visited. It seemed to be trying to drum up business as a restaurant with a short menu displayed on one of the windows. On the opposite window, a small card with the words 'Vacancies, Inquire Within', sounded faintly desperate.

Alan opened the gate into the cemetery, walked along a winding path flanked by trees and sat on a bench next to a bin full of dead flowers. He thought of the station waiting room near to the house where his mum and Peggy lived. He had slept in there one January night when his mother's car had failed to get through the deep snow. In the early morning, the milk train had taken him a few miles down the track and stopped so he could jump off and walk across the fields in the dark. The snow was at least three feet deep and he remembered how muffled and quiet everything was and how alive and sharp he felt under the sky, clear as black glass.

It had taken him quite a while to wake his mother that early morning. He seemed to bang for ages with numb fists on the back door. Eventually a light came on upstairs and then his mother had appeared in a checked woollen dressing gown that reminded him of Rupert Bear. They had sat in the kitchen close to the boiler, drinking hot sweet tea. She had asked him how school was going and what he was thinking of doing afterwards, as he would be leaving in six months. It seemed to be their first conversation as adults and after Alan had answered all her questions he felt bold enough to ask one of his own, one he had wanted to ask her all his childhood.

'Why did you leave?'

She put her feet to warm on the small glass hatch in the boiler.

'Ah, I needed to escape from your father.'

She went on to explain that Alan's father had become impossible, so demanding, so controlling. He would make a ridiculous fuss over nothing. She asked if he remembered their neighbour Mr Kablinski? He nodded. She reminded him that he had been a prisoner of war who had lost his wife to cancer within a year of being reunited with her. He had been gentle and cultured and so knowledgeable about growing vegetables. She remembered him telling her about the fat cabbages and black cherries in his garden back home. They only ever spoke to each other in the garden over the fence. Sometimes he would make her good strong Polish coffee or she would make him good strong English tea. He never drank the tea, just kept adding sugar and stirred it endlessly until it was cold. She had found his coffee too treacly and after a few sips put it on the kitchen windowsill. They stopped swopping drinks and just exchanged cigarettes. She used to hear his music playing through the wall, mainly piano. Sometimes he sang with a thin reedy voice. She looked up at Alan. 'It was like a sad seagull, you used to say.'

Alan smiled.

'I don't remember the singing, but I do remember him. He was tall and fair with a frowning forehead even when he smiled. He made me a wooden whistle and an engine with a Union Jack on the side in coloured pencil. I loved that.'

His mother shrugged and reminded Alan that his father had thrown the engine on the fire in one of his tempers. She had taken it straight off and convinced Alan the brown mark was from the coal burning inside. His father had said she was carrying on behind his back and she had been forbidden to talk to 'that damn Pole'. She had thought that ridiculous, as poor Mr Kablinski was just lonely and sad. Alan's father had been such a bully of a man, so insistent, pushy and self-righteous. In bed he had been a disaster, huffing and puffing his way through in a few seconds.

'Mother, please!'

'Sorry darling. It's just I know you found the whole thing difficult and I'm simply trying to explain why it happened.'

'But what about Peggy? I always felt she lured you away, brainwashed you to go and live with her.'

Alan's mother sighed. Peggy had started visiting as she was lonely and like many others after the war had lost her sense of purpose. She had adored being in the Land Army, loved the outdoor life, the company of women and the feeling of being useful. It had been Peggy who had looked after them all when they went to dances. She drove them in a great big lorry and kept an eye out for the girls overdoing the cider and being taken advantage of. After the war, she went back home to look after her mother, where she set up a Girl Guide troop and volunteered at the local hospital. But it was all rather tame and dull. She was restless and nothing seemed quite enough for her.

Alan's mother had been pleased when Peggy started visiting, as they had many shared memories and could chat and laugh for hours.

'It was only after the incident with your father that she suggested I might actually go and live with her.'

'Incident?'

'Yes. Well, you see, I was pregnant.'

Apparently, Alan's father was particularly angry one night and they had argued about some silly thing. Maybe he had had a bit to drink. Alan's mother had wanted to have a bath, get away from him, but he wouldn't let it go. He followed her onto the landing and started pushing her, jabbing her arm with his finger, then something seemed to snap and he was shouting for her to go, leave the house, get out. His mother didn't think he really meant to but he pushed her down the stairs. She remembered slithering awkwardly on the wood and carpet, her dressing gown catching on the metal treads. Then she was lying in the hall face-to-face with the skirting board and it seemed difficult to move.

'Anyway, I lost the baby.'

Peggy offered her a refuge. She had a large comfortable house and was lonely. Most of her friends had jumped into marriage after the war and rushed off to various suburbs to breed away the years of hardship. Alan's mother had done the same. 'Marry in haste, repent at leisure.'

Alan saw that a faint light was appearing beyond the Ajax and Lux flakes on the windowsill. He felt unable to say anything. He heard the distant hoot of a train.

His mother stood up.

'Your father exaggerated the whole lesbian thing to explain away the shame of me leaving him.'

Alan noted the word 'exaggerated' rather than 'made up' but still felt unable to speak. He stared at his reflection in the kitchen window, snowy fields stretching across his shoulders and early morning creeping along his neck.

'You must be tired, Alan. I'll get some blankets and you can snatch some sleep on the sofa. I'm going to get a bit of shut-eye before it gets light. I'm so glad we've had this chance to talk.'

She put her hands on his shoulders and kissed the top of his head.

'It's good to see you, it really is.'

She padded towards the door in her thick socks.

His voice sounded croaky, the question coming out more loudly than he had intended.

'The baby, the baby that you lost, did you know, did you know what it was?'

'It was a girl.'

'A sister.'

A voice broke into his thoughts and Marie was shouting and waving from outside the newsagent's. She crossed the road and came through the gate to the cemetery. He smiled and waved back as she ran towards him up the path that twisted through the graves. A black woolly glove ruffled his hair and brought him back to the present.

'Sorry I was so long but the man in the sweet shop remembered the railway and we got chatting. It was so interesting. I bought a newspaper. Have an aniseed twist and I'll tell you what he said.'

VALERIE

Valerie Jones had finally got rid of a difficult parent. The meeting about his truanting daughter had taken over an hour. She understood that the poor man was struggling after his wife had left him to bring up a fourteen-year-old girl on his own and he was finding it hard. After twenty minutes, she found herself repeating the same things, offering the same advice, suggesting the same strategies over again. The father wanted to keep talking. He wanted to keep going over the same points as if a different speck of possibility might emerge just by discussion. So, talk they did, until Valerie Jones was able to conclude the meeting by suggesting a further one the following week.

It was late on a Friday afternoon and Valerie had been trying to make time to see DI Wilson all week, but had failed. She bustled about her office making sure she had all her relevant files for the weekend, various letters and pieces of paper. She stuffed everything into a large holdall, grabbed her scarf and coat, locked her office and hurried down the corridor. She arrived at Wilson's office just as Arthur Simmons was locking the door.

'He's just left. Gone to the boozer, the one at the end of the road. Only a couple of minutes ago.'

Valerie Jones was in two minds. She was really keen to ask Wilson about the photos but also a bit reluctant to go to the pub on her own. It was not something she would normally do. She also wondered if Wilson would mind her intrusion, since he was off duty.

'Oh, what the hell.' She decided to brave the pub and as soon as she'd opened the door she saw Wilson standing at the bar. He seemed genuinely pleased to see her and smiled welcomingly.

'Mrs Jones, what a pleasant surprise. What will you have to drink?'

The pub seemed to pride itself on being insulated from the outside world. There were thick greyish net curtains at the windows, framed with even heavier velvet curtains that looked as though they hadn't been disturbed for a couple of years and would have channels of dust in the creases if anyone tried to pull them. The walls were covered in a thickly textured paper and the spongy carpet was highly coloured and multi-patterned. A gauze of smoke hung above everything.

Valerie Jones sat on the end of a pink velvet bench that took up a corner of the saloon bar nearest the door. She had taken off her coat but still had her scarf knotted round her neck. It didn't feel entirely appropriate to totally relax. She closed her eyes briefly. It felt good to sit down after a very busy day dealing with badly behaved children and difficult parents. She slipped her shoes off under the table hoping no one would see. There was a phone booth in the corridor next to the toilets and Valerie decided she would phone her husband in a minute to tell him she would be late. He played squash on a Friday night and could get some fish and chips on his way home. She sighed a small sigh, thinking that there was one less thing to worry about. Maybe she could get some food here, as she wouldn't feel like cooking for just herself later.

'Please call me Ray,' Wilson had said when he asked her what she would like to drink. He was standing at the bar still wearing his raincoat, which was a bit creased. How old was he? He must be at least ten years older than me she thought – probably in his mid-forties.

He set the drinks down carefully with a packet of peanuts. His pint of bitter slopped slightly onto the table but her lager and lime was intact. She noted it had been put in a ladies' glass and wondered briefly if he had requested that. The thought made her a little self-conscious, as if they could be a man and woman out socially. But I need to talk to him about work, she told herself. I would have been just as happy in the staffroom. It doesn't matter, for goodness sake, so stop getting all worked up. She could hear her husband's voice in her head. Just relax, you're having a drink after work, that's all.

'Cheers.' He gulped half the glass in one go. 'God, I needed that.'

'Cheers. Thank you for my drink.' She sipped at her lager and, feeling more at ease, put a small handful of peanuts in her mouth.

'Ray, I wanted to ask you about the photos, you know the ones that Arthur, Mr Simmons, the caretaker, gave you of Pamela Webb. I've been meaning to speak to you for the last couple of days but I haven't seemed to find a moment. I didn't want to go home for the weekend not knowing. It's been worrying me. I haven't seen them myself, but Arthur told me the nature of them.

She felt a bit awkward again and hadn't quite known how to phrase her question. She was also aware of the couple sitting at the other end of the bench, so spoke softly. Ray leaned towards her so he could hear properly and their heads were quite close across the table. Fortunately, the other couple stood up to leave so Valerie sat back, relaxed her shoulders and spoke again.

'Have the photos helped the enquiry into Pamela's disappearance? Are there any connections?'

Ray finished his beer and briefly wiped his mouth.

'We did follow up the photos, Valerie. We found out who took them and paid a visit but it seems as far as Pamela was concerned it was a one-off. She did a bit of modelling for a couple of unsavoury characters but didn't see them again. It was offered as a way to earn money and she didn't realise she would be required to strip. We know she went with her friend, Caroline, and we've spoken to her. She was quite upset, poor kid, felt she'd let Pamela down in some way. We haven't yet found a link with her disappearance and this seedy little incident.'

'So it's just coincidence that one of the caretakers spotted her in the photo?'

'It seems so.'

'Has anyone else in the school seen them?'

'Just Miss Lloyd.'

'So, no further leads on Pamela?'

'I'm afraid not.'

'What do they do with the photos?'

'Sell them, probably in pubs like this, locally, and for bigger money. There are always sick people willing to pay for this kind of stuff unfortunately.'

'Is it usually pictures of girls?'

'I'm not an expert in the field but young girls seem to cater for a large part of the market, although of course there's quite a different but strong demand for pictures of young boys.'

Valerie shuddered at this new horrible train of thought and wanted to change the subject. She felt hungry as a young girl walked past with two plates of food and a large bottle of ketchup on a tray.

'Would you mind if I had something to eat? I've had a really busy day and didn't have much lunch.'

'I'm feeling a bit peckish myself so I might join you. I'll go and get a couple of menus. There's not a huge choice but I can recommend the chicken in a basket.'

Valerie smiled and loosened her scarf. She felt suddenly relaxed, and so pleased it was Friday. Tomorrow she would stay in bed, have a cup of tea, read her book, listen to the radio, do some shopping, please herself. Saturday bliss. She looked towards the windows, and in her own warmth and contentment thought of all the dark streets outside where the Friday-night traffic was starting to ease off. Where in all of these suburbs, the housing estates, the railway stations, the old churches, the disused factories, the empty parks and closed shops, was Pamela Webb?

SALLY

Cathy had insisted they come, had offered to pick Sally up and lent her an amber necklace. Sally had not wanted to come to this party but in the absence of anything else going on had reluctantly agreed. Then another friend told her it was where Sean lived and she was more interested. He was one of the men on Sally's list of 'attractive possibilities'. She had seen him at college standing in a doorway or sitting at the far end of the bar always on the edge of things. He was dark, tall and usually wore a heavy coat and thin scarf.

She had been reading *The Virgin and the Gypsy* by D. H. Lawrence and thought of him as the gypsy. Cathy had teased her about this and continued to make fun of her as they parked outside a row of Victorian artisan cottages.

'We might see Sean's caravan in the garden. It's probably painted canary yellow!'

'You've got to admit he's good-looking.'

'Not my type.'

They entered through the doorway of the end house but quickly discovered you could enter through any of the doors and still finish up in the wide garden where the bonfire was. The garden was the width of eight houses, all the dividing fences having been taken away. A couple of posts and a gate remained, a reminder of earlier divisions, but redundant in this large open space.

Cathy and Sally stood quite close to the fire, enjoying the heat and watching the clean yellow flames licking the sky. It was cold, dry and clear. At intervals, two drunk men made half-hearted attempts to set off fireworks, so every fifteen minutes or so a small rocket would lurch into the sky, or a golden rain balanced on the fence would splutter into life. No one was really watching.

A group of friends sat smoking dope on a battered old sofa propped up against a garden shed with no roof. They shouted 'ooh' and 'aah' intermittently, but never seemed to synchronise the noise with any firework going off. This lack of timing was sending them into increasingly uncontrollable bouts of laughter.

Sally was interested in the variety of the eight identical houses and started to explore. Some were uncared for, messy and dirty with stained kitchen sinks and piles of randomly placed mattresses, but one was immaculate. Everything in the kitchen was yellow and blue, all the walls and furniture painted in different shades of bright cheerful colours. A cornflower dresser held rows of willow-pattern plates next to decorative tins of treacle toffee and Scottish shortbread. Blue check curtains hung at the window and a wooden clothes drier stood next to a fire that was actually lit. Sally smiled with admiration at the care someone had taken in this welcoming room. At the last house, she walked into the kitchen where she found Sean sitting at the table. He looked up and smiled.

'Hallo, I know your face from somewhere.'

'Yes, college probably.'

'Would you like to try some of this? It's very good'

'What is it?'

'It's called halva, it's very sweet and delicious. I got it from the Greek shop.'

It was white and crumbly in her mouth and, yes, certainly sweet and delicious.

'It's good. I like it.'

'Have some more.'

Sally couldn't believe her luck, to have walked into the last house and seen Sean. She had been wondering if he would even be at the party.

'Do you live here? Is this your kitchen?'

She sat on a nearby stool, the halva melting on her tongue. Apparently Sean had moved in last June and spent the fantastic long hot summer mostly in the huge tangled garden. The houses were condemned and they only had six months left of the tenancy.

'So will they be pulled down?'

'Afraid so.'

He moved to the draining board and put a couple of smeary glasses on the table.

'Try this, it's a liqueur. The Greek shop again. Quite strong.'

She swallowed a large mouthful and her throat burned.

'God, it tastes like something you add to oil paints. It's awful.'

'Yes, isn't it, have another.'

Sally winced as she downed the drink in one huge burning gulp.

'Should we throw our glasses into the fireplace now?'

'Probably, but seeing as we only have the two...'

A fair-haired woman appeared in the doorway wearing a long, creased green velvet dress and looking to Sally as if she had just stepped out of a Pre-Raphaelite painting.

'Sean, why are there so many people in the garden?'

It seemed as if she had just woken up. Her hair was knotted and her eyes were bleary. She opened them wide and kept blinking as if to understand more clearly what was going on around her. Sean reminded her it was Bonfire Night and someone must have decided to have a party. He offered her a drink, which she refused by shaking her head.

'Not that awful Greek stuff. My head still hurts at the thought of it. I'm going to make some tea.'

She turned and smiled at Sally.

'Hallo, I'm Angie. Would you like some tea?'

Having put the kettle on the gas, Angie sat at the table, took out a tin of tobacco and started rolling a thin cigarette. She looked at Sally sideways.

'Are you a student? At the art college?'

'I was, but I started teaching in September.'

'Anywhere round here?'

Sally told her the name of the school.

Angie opened a drawer looking for matches.

'Fucking mice get in everywhere.'

'Here.'

Sean threw her a lighter and she lit her cigarette shakily then sat back, delicately picking tobacco from her teeth.

'Isn't that the school where the kid has gone missing? I saw it on the telly. Are there any leads, any suspects?'

'I don't know. They give us various bits of information but no more than you get in the newspapers or on the telly.'

As Angie leaned forward frowning, Sally studied her large forehead and white skin. She could see a thin blue vein at her temple and thought Angie looked frail and unhealthy.

'I have an idea. It came to me on Wednesday when I was digging in the allotment. We've got one on the hill, you know, near the station. It's Pippa's really but she lets us use a bit of her land. I was thinking about that poor kid. That photo they show on the telly with her smiling face and little Alice band had burned itself into my brain. It got me thinking that allotments are a perfect place to hide a body, with so much digging going on. All that freshly turned earth, so where would you start to look? And it could happen without you knowing. I mean someone could put a body under the earth where I planted the potatoes. As long as it was deep enough I wouldn't check. If I thought the earth looked a bit disturbed I would think a dog had been at it. Anyway, I've started to keep my eye on the people at the allotment. You never know.'

Sean snorted, partly in a derisory way and partly because he was trying to light his rather over-sized spliff and had breathed in too quickly. Angie sensed she was being laughed at and turned to Sally again. She had completely forgotten she was making tea.

'As you're an art teacher, can I show you my paintings? They're upstairs in the bedroom.'

The bedroom was freezing and as Angie clicked on a dim lamp Sally could see the walls were covered in Indian bedspreads and the floor was more or less filled by a large mattress on which was heaped a pile of patchwork cushions. Angie passed her the canvases, one by one, shining a torch on them in the gloom. The paintings were wispy and detailed fantasies that for all their whimsy and soft colours had a sense of cruelty.

'It's all from my imagination,' Angie whispered. 'Do you like them?'

Sally didn't like them at all and struggled to say something positive. Angie looked straight at her intensely, waiting for an answer. She was like a child. It was both irritating and compelling.

'Very imaginative. I like all the detail.'

Angie patted the mattress inviting Sally to sit down. 'Pippa likes them. I gave her one for her birthday.'

It transpired that Pippa lived in the house next door and was the creator of the colourful kitchen.

Sally was glad of her coat. Angie had wrapped herself in a blanket and proceeded to unravel the complexities of her life with Sean. It seemed she shared him with Pippa.

'We appeal to the different sides of him. Pippa has the brains and I've got the beauty. She is practical and I am an artist. I mean, I do admire her. She's so together – she can make furniture, and she knows about electricity and things like that. She even has a proper job, social work I think, so can buy things like a car. You might have seen that 2CV outside, green, well that's Pippa's.

'We'll be thrown out of here in a few months. I was at my Nan's yesterday, she lives up at the Palace and I've noticed some old prefabs, most of them are empty. So I got to wondering whether we could move there but it turns out they're gonna be knocked down too. We might have to go further afield, but God knows where. Pippa's managed to get a plot for one of those new self-build houses, on the hill opposite the allotments.'

'Yes I've heard of them. They sound interesting.'

'Yeah, well practical old Pippa got her name down early so she's in.'

Later, after Cathy had driven her home, Sally sat on her bed wrapped in an eiderdown and considered the evening. A mug of tea steamed into the cold air on her bedside table.

There was an attraction about the life that Sean and Angie lived, drifting around in a world free from responsibility, choosing to visit the allotment on a sunny day, then the museum or library when it rained. They lived the lives of students but without the studying, and used the college as their social club. It wasn't too difficult getting in past the porters with a crowd, or into the various music gigs through the toilet window.

But this dreamy freedom had a different side. Uncertainty would run through your life, a constant seam of tension about where you would live next month or next week. You could strike lucky with a large old house recently vacated but still in good nick, or have to put up with damp and cold and mice. There was no guarantee of anything; a lack of money, lack of possessions and the lack of home. Where would they live once the houses were demolished? Having to go to the swimming baths to have a hot shower was not always practical. It had all been relatively easy during the long hot summer but as each week of winter passed it got harder.

Sally knew that Sean and Angie's life seemed appealing because she missed the cushioning of her student days now that she had the reality and grind of a job. Her day was tightly structured with bus timetables, lesson timetables and homework timetables. She had to be alert and organised, she had to be a teacher, but she didn't quite feel like one yet.

Sally switched off the light and lay listening to the occasional car passing on the heath. So that was Sean crossed off the list of possible boyfriends. She had seen Jeff a few days ago and crossed him off the list too. There was something indecent about the haste with which he had embraced the world of work. You had to be suspicious of someone who wears jeans and long hair one day then suddenly appears in a suit the next. A suit! That was going too far. Most men Sally knew would start with a jacket, maybe progress to a tie after a few months then gradually work up to a suit within a decade. But Jeff seemed to have fast forwarded into conformity at an alarming rate. He didn't look so attractive with short hair either, and his shoes were too shiny, thought Sally. Then she fell asleep.

PAMELA

It's arranged now. We're going to meet at lunchtime by the gates, as if we're going home for our dinner. He is not sure how many puppies there are, perhaps three or four, but I can choose the one I like best. We need to go as soon as possible because the old man might get rid of them. He has been grumbling about them getting in the way and saying he might drown them. So we need to be quick. I don't want him to kill them.

So Monday is the best day.

He told me not to worry about French and geography, although I still am worried because I have never bunked off before. It's only two lessons, he said, and he will write me a note to say I've been at the dentist. It's worth it if I can save the puppies or at least one. Maybe I could take two. I did mention it to mum and she didn't seem too keen but I'm sure she'll come round.

I think we have to walk there but it's not too far and I don't mind.

I mustn't tell anyone. I don't want to tell anyone.

ALAN

On Sunday, Alan and Marie visited the site of Lordship Lane station. Alan had some old photos that showed an ornate building with three arches and a number of tall slim chimneys. He also had a view from the 1920s showing a colonnaded bridge crossing the road and a rickety trolleybus climbing the hill just outside the station.

Alan took a few photos of a new estate now built on the site. It was difficult to locate where the station building had actually been. Was it parallel to the road or at an angle to it? He was now keen to see if a bridge he remembered from his childhood as being behind the station at some distance was still there.

Looking at his map, Alan realised they had to go up a steep hill to a high ridge and the road that was on a level with the Crystal Palace. Marie groaned at the prospect. She cycled about halfway then got off her bike and pushed it. Alan overtook her and waited at the top. Marie was quite breathless as they pushed their bikes along the ridge looking for a path to the bridge. It was actually signposted and after locking their bikes they took a steep path that led through thick trees whose roots almost formed haphazard steps. It led them down to a bridge that crossed a ravine full of bushes flanked with more trees.

Alan took several photos.

'I remember being on this bridge before.'

Alan explained that his father had brought him there as a child when they visited his new school for the first time. Neither of them had found it an easy experience. His father was obviously intimidated by the interview with the headmaster, all poshness and protocol, and Alan had just been upset and confused at the direction his life was taking. There was a good pub at the top of the road. Alan remembered his dad parking the Wolsey outside and bringing him out a bag of crisps while he went inside for a quick gulp of whisky. After that he had been brought along to this bridge. His father thought he would like to see the trains.

'And did you see any trains?'

'Yes. We stood here for quite a while, not saying much, and it was a bit awkward. Dad was explaining things about the school, going over what the headmaster had just said, trying to reassure me I suppose, but I was in a fog of sadness. Then we heard it, the sound of the engine, the chug, followed by the steam appearing above the trees and then it came straight towards us here. I can still see it. I rushed to the other side of the bridge and watched it disappear on its way up to Crystal Palace, the chug getting fainter, the steam thinner and then it was gone. All I could think to say to my dad was 'When will I see Mummy?'

Marie touched his arm.

'I'm so glad I didn't have to go away to school.'

"Come on, let's get moving. There's a decent pub at the bottom of this path, so we can have a bite to eat and warm up.'

Later that evening they were both drinking tea in Alan's sitting room. Marie had started to organise all the information on the old railway. She had brought a large sketchbook and sat in front of Alan's gas fire, wearing knitted slippers, and arranged the photos with the newspaper articles and the maps until she was satisfied.

'What do you think?'

'Good, it looks good.'

Marie reached for the glue, her lips slightly pursed as she carefully stuck everything down and finished by making a label with the name of each station painted in navy blue. She put the sketchbook to one side to dry and picked up one of the local history books she had got from the library. Marie was becoming seriously interested in the whole railway project and reading whatever she could get hold of.

'Listen to this, Alan. Samuel Pepys went with his wife and servant to see the gypsies at Lambeth where she had her fortune told. It is commonly believed this was Gipsy Hill, a densely forested area in those days. The date is 11th August 1668.'

Marie put the book down.

'It may have been hot and sunny. I can imagine them on horseback, slowly descending the slope under dappled trees. No houses, no railway, just dense forest. The city of London a small faraway place. I wonder if the gypsy read cards or had a crystal ball. Were crystal balls invented then? Are you listening to me?'

'Yes, Samuel Pepys.'

Alan flicked the pages of an exhibition catalogue at one end of the threadbare sofa and didn't appear to be really listening.

'I can't get that bridge we saw today out of my mind.'

Alan put the catalogue down on the table next to Marie. She looked up, not really wanting to be disturbed, but asked dutifully.

'What are you thinking?'

'You know the Pissarro painting?'

'Oh, you mean the one we saw in the exhibition, the one they weren't certain about, the "probably Penge" Station?'

'Yeah, that one.'

'Well, what about it?'

'Look at the painting.'

'Let me see.'

She looked again at the slope of land and the bare green hill, the train steaming towards the viewer in the painting. The houses were scattered, new and raw on the hillside, standing out on the not yet cluttered landscape.

'Alan, you know I had to get off my bike and walk up the hill this morning? Then we had to walk down to the railway bridge. Both times it felt pretty steep to me.'

'And so?'

'Could this "probably Penge" Station be Lordship Lane Station, looking from the bridge where we were today? It would explain the sharp rise of the land on the right.'

Alan screwed up his face and looked sceptical.

'What about all the trees, so dense, so many?'

Marie took the catalogue and peered closely at the painting.

'They've had a hundred years to grow, and look at the left-hand side. There's a tree just like the later ones. The growth is starting.'

Alan thought of his childhood vision of the steam train rushing towards him: could he remember trees on the embankment then? He had an overall impression of openness, much more sky, but there could have been smaller trees, the ratio of tree and sky could have been more equal. He closed his eyes and concentrated, but all he could see was the train and this was from a lower height, his face closer to the iron of the bridge. He remembered that he had worn no gloves and that his hands were cold. His father had given him a half-crown earlier, which he felt for every so often in his coat pocket. It felt like a talisman from home and he wasn't sure if he would spend it. He couldn't remember anything more about the railway or the bridge. He looked at Marie.

'You may be right. By process of elimination there can't be many more stations it could be, but there needs to be proof, something more definite.'

Marie grabbed the catalogue from him and moved across to the lamp on the table.

'Yes, look, Alan, look at the houses in the background.'

He hunched next to her in the brighter pool of light.

'What about them?

'We may have passed one of them this morning. They could still be there. If we can identify at least one of them it would prove this was Pissarro's station.'

Alan squinted at the houses in the painting, scrutinising the details of roofs and gables, the vague dabs of windows.

'Good God you're right. You're brilliant. You're gorgeous.'

He kissed her neck and jumped up.

'I want to go now. I can't wait. I want to check the houses.'

'Stop acting silly. You won't see a thing at this time of night.'

They arranged that Alan should go on his bike first thing in the morning, and Marie would open up the shop and stay there until he returned. She had no clear college commitments or nothing that couldn't be dealt with in the afternoon.

Alan couldn't sleep. He kept trying to picture the houses on the hill Marie and he had cycled past. He had not taken in his surroundings and had just concentrated on following her woollen coat and black beret, concerned at her breathlessness and laughing when she eventually gave up and walked. He had forged ahead and waited for her at the top, scornful of her protests at not having any gears. It was the image of Marie pushing her bike towards him, red in the face and puffing that filled Alan's mind. He couldn't see any houses at all.

VALERIE

Valerie Jones almost tripped over Sharon's foot as she fumbled for her key in her bag. She hadn't expected anyone to be sitting outside her office so early. She was surprised to see Sharon there at all; usually Valerie had to seek her out.

'Morning, Sharon, do you want to see me?'

The girl gave a sharp nod and stood up, banging her bag against the chair.

Valerie pushed open the door to her office.

'Come in and take a seat.'

Sharon sat down and seemed to dissolve on the desk. She put her head on her arms, and her shoulders started to shake. Sobbing sounds came from the depths of her woollen scarf.

Valerie put a hand on her back.

'What is it, Sharon, what's wrong?'

'I don't know what to do, I don't know who to tell, I don't know where to go.'

She lifted her head and looked at Valerie, her nose running and eyes smudges of black.

'What shall I do?'

Valerie asked Sharon to tell her what had happened to upset her so much, and advised her to take some deep breaths and start at the beginning.

'I hate the bastard. Why doesn't he leave us alone, stay away. He's evil.'

Valerie noticed a grey and yellow bruise on Sharon's neck that spread towards her ear. She asked if Sharon was talking about her dad. She nodded and continued.

'He just turns up drunk out of his head and tries to get money off my mum. She doesn't have any so he tries to beat it out of her. He's fat and strong. I try to stop him so he turns on me. He stinks, he shouts and the kids are awake. I don't want them to see. Bastard.'

Her face was wet, and she ran the back of her hands across her eyes, smearing more mascara.

Valerie opened a drawer in her desk and handed Sharon some tissues. Sharon's shoulders were still shaking and she was temporarily unable to speak.

Valerie told Sharon she would go to the staffroom and make her a cup of tea. She returned a few minutes later to find her sitting upright and looking out of the window into the more or less empty car park. She had wiped her face and looked more like her usual self. The storm of anger had swept through her and subsided. She sipped the sweet tea urgently, then gradually, once the mug was empty, she started to talk. Sharon didn't look at Valerie, she just reeled off bulletins of information, facts and a few dates. There was no emotion on the surface, no swear words or insults, just the bare bones of what had happened. Valerie asked about the bruises, but Sharon hadn't even realised they were there. They talked about short and long-term solutions. Eventually Sharon seemed calmer, and although slightly soothed by Valerie's matter-of-fact approach, was still flattened and resigned and looked tense and defeated.

'Did you get any sleep last night Sharon?'

'No, 'cos I thought he might come back. Then it got light. The kids were in my bed. They were scared to be on their own. Mum was flat out.'

Valerie said she would phone Sharon's mum to have a chat and suggested that she should go and get some sleep in the medical room for a few hours. After that, she could either go to afternoon lessons or go home, depending on how she felt.

For the first time that morning, Sharon lifted her head and looked Valerie straight in the eyes.

'Thank you, Miss.' She looked exhausted.

At the start of the lunch break Valerie looked in on the medical room. Sharon was still lying on the bed but she opened her eyes when she heard the door. Corridor noises spilled into the darkened room.

'Feeling better?'

Sharon nodded and sat up, her clothes more creased than ever but with a slightly clearer face. She swung her feet off the bed and started to put on her shoes.

'Sharon, is there a friend I can fetch? Someone to keep you company for the rest of the day, look after you a bit?'

'Not really. I mean the girls in my class are OK but I don't hang out with them outside school. Nick is my main friend but he's been a bit off recently.'

Sharon stood up and tried to smooth out her skirt, picking off blanket hairs with her fingernails. Valerie pulled the curtains apart, letting in the grey light so they could both see better.

'How do you mean "off"?'

'He often misses school, always has done, although I'm not sure why, but he's been saying strange things recently.'

'Such as?'

'I dunno. He keeps talking about medals. I mean I know he's interested in them. He was going on last term about getting his bronze. A few weeks back he seemed really excited about something. When I asked him what was up he just smiled and said he'd finally got his gold. He couldn't take this stupid grin off his face, kept talking about it. His actual words were, "Oh yes I've finally got my Olympic Gold."'

It was this part of the conversation that Valerie Jones repeated to DI Wilson later that day.

She told him that Sharon had spoken to her quite openly. She seemed to have let her guard drop momentarily and all her defensive layers had disappeared. Maybe it was because she had been sleeping, or because she had come to Valerie for help earlier in the day and felt more relaxed. Anyway, it had been short-lived. Valerie had seen her a few minutes ago and when questioned she had clammed up and was her usual bristling, hostile self. She asked Sharon again about Nick but she refused to cooperate, said she didn't know anything about his life outside school, and that she couldn't tell her anything.

Wilson frowned and said, 'Couldn't or wouldn't?'

'Obviously I can't be sure, but I think Sharon's told us all she knows. I don't think she would withhold important information, not in a case as serious as this.'

'Assuming she understood what was and was not important. Also Sharon has been known to withhold information.'

'What do you mean?'

'The first time I interviewed her, I asked her if she knew Pamela.'

'Yes, and?'

'She said she didn't, even acted offended as if being friends with a younger girl was beneath her.'

'Did she know her then?'

Wilson told Valerie it was Sharon who had got Pamela into the naked modelling. Her little mate Caroline had come to tell him what had happened. She had gone along too, although neither of them had realised that 'modelling' would involve taking their clothes off. Caroline had refused to do it but Pamela had been more cooperative.

Valerie thought of the evening spent in the pub when she had asked Wilson about the photos. She also remembered Arthur Simmons sitting in her office with the photos tucked into the pocket of his overalls. She was glad she hadn't seen them. When she asked Wilson if he had spoken to Sharon he said that he had and that she had been put under pressure to find 'new young girls'; she herself had been involved in the same sordid business since she was twelve apparently.

'You mean modelling naked?'

'Yeah, her dad set it up, an arrangement to pay off debts or something like that, but poor Sharon didn't look young enough any more, she had become too womanly, too developed, so she was sent off to find replacements. It was made clear to her she had to be successful, and not finding anyone was not an option. She was frightened of these men, so obviously they had threatened her.'

Valerie sighed and went into more detail about Sharon's early morning visit and how upset she had been. She related some of Sharon's descriptions of her violent

father and the difficulties the family found themselves
in. Wilson had been looking at Valerie as he listened to
her talking and noticing the way her thin blonde hair
was escaping from its ponytail, several strands of which
were curving round her neck. His focus changed and
shifted to the old map of London directly behind her
head, where a railway line was running down towards
her collar. It was the old Crystal Palace line ending at
a large black rectangle, the station, just behind Valerie's
shoulder.

'What is it?'

'Isn't it amazing how you can sit in front of something
day in and day out and not really take it in. I studied it
on the first day but since then it's become familiar, like
wallpaper.'

Valerie turned to look.

'This is an out-of-date map, 1928 to be precise, so
I haven't thought to use it, considered it irrelevant. I've
been working on this current one over here.'

He pointed at a map covered with notes, photos and
labels showing dates and times, then turned back.

'Look, here is the old Crystal Palace railway track. It
comes across from Greenwich to Nunhead then heads
south.'

'"From the nuns head to the screaming Alice," my
Nan used to say. Funny, I'd forgotten that old phrase
until just now.'

'Sounds like Lewis Carroll.'

'Yes.'

'The Palace burned down didn't it?'

'Yes, it did.'

Wilson was obviously preoccupied with some new thought. He ran his finger along the thin black snake that was the railway line. The rust coloured contour lines were very close together.

He turned to her. 'There is the tunnel before the railway finally reaches Crystal Palace. You can see there where the black line becomes dotted. It emerged on what was the actual station, a colossal building. There are two tunnels, the one that comes out on Crystal Palace Parade and another one that is in the woods.'

Valerie looked up at him.

'Surely they were searched in September when all the local railways were checked?'

'They were searched all right. I did it myself. It's funny, you can come up the hill from Penge or Norwood or Sydenham, any number of roads all leading to what? There's just a great big space. It's a let-down and a disappointment. You reach the top and see a big chunk of grass, a couple of radio towers and a bus terminus. Such an anti-climax compared to a palace of glass.'

Valerie swallowed, unsure whether her imminent question would be an insult to DI Wilson, or Ray. She couldn't be certain of his age and didn't know when the Crystal Palace burned down.

'Did you see it, the Crystal Palace, before it burned down?'

'I must have done, but I don't really remember it. I was just a kid. I saw it after the fire though – my dad and I came specially on the bus.'

Wilson described seeing a huge twisted metal carcass, rubble everywhere and a strong smell, the combined stench of burning and damp. There had been a persistent drizzle all that day. His dad had been horrified and they had walked along the Parade several times just to take in the scale of it all.

'For me, though, as a boy passionate about railways, the most exciting thing as we walked up and down was on the other side of the road.'

Wilson smiled and then said in a loud voice like a platform announcement.

'The Crystal Palace Higher Level Railway Station.'

The other side of the road.

He thought back to the day he and his cousin had thrown bricks in the old station building after the cinema visit. He remembered how they had reached the station by walking under the road. As a boy it was nothing special, just a cut through to the more interesting station, and he had used that way many times. Now he thought about it, the space was wide, obviously at least the width of the road and had an unusual ceiling, like a church. Maybe this had been the place Aunty Lily had sheltered in during the war. He had never really understood how you could fit musicians and bunk beds into the two train tunnels, which seemed far too narrow. Yes, it made sense; it would have provided a generous air-raid shelter. The council had properly secured this tunnel under the road about ten years ago with metal doors with small grilles so no one could get through. Wilson hadn't been there since he was a boy and had almost forgotten about it, but looking at the old map today had jogged his memory.

He spoke to Valerie again.

'The station is long gone. I was up at the Palace a few weeks back, to investigate suspected arson.'

Wilson went on to explain how an old gypsy had lived in a caravan beyond the prefabs on the old station site. He had been a bit of a local legend. Some older folks remembered him playing his violin in the tavern in Lordship Lane from before the war. In those days, the girls had been after him with his good looks and dark curly hair. During the war he disappeared for a few years then turned up again living rough in the old railway station. When that was pulled down, he towed a caravan onto the site and somehow managed to evade the local authorities. In the end, it seemed they just ignored him.

Valerie looked concerned.

'So, was it arson?'

'Don't think so, but it's hard to be certain.'

Wilson explained that a woman in one of the prefabs had seen the blaze but by the time she'd phoned for the fire brigade the caravan had exploded. The gypsy's dog, that had been barking constantly and alerted the woman in the first place, was freed by the fire and ran clear. Local kids had been scared of the old gypsy and his dog and generally stayed away. The woman in the prefab had tried to help out but he wasn't having any of it. So he was pretty much left alone. Wilson stood up.

'His name was Stanley.'

Valerie felt that she was being dismissed so also stood and put her coat on. Wilson locked the filing cabinet and snapped his briefcase shut. He seemed to remember why she had come.

'I need to talk to Nick and Sharon again. In fact, I'd been planning to do so tomorrow as Nick seems linked in some way I can't put my finger on. I keep going through his file but nothing is jumping out at me.'

He held the door open for Valerie.

'"Olympic Gold." What does that mean?'

ALAN

He had eaten half a piece of toast and swallowed a mug of tea in his small kitchen with the light on at about 7.30am, keeping the ring on the gas stove burning as the only form of heat, since he was in too much of a hurry to use anything else. As he stepped out of his front door, breath cold on the air, and up the steps onto the heath, there was a grey strip of light making its way across the horizon. He stopped at the nearest newsagent's in the village, the only shop with a welcoming light at this early hour, to buy a roll of 36 colour film.

Thankfully it was dry, but cold, and slightly overcast. Alan cycled along the side of the heath, noticing the lights in the factory behind the pub and clusters of women waiting outside, ready to clock on for the early shift. He liked the fact that a factory was there in among all these grand houses and wondered not for the first time what they made there. One day he would find out. He then dropped down towards Lewisham, past windows where people were still sleeping, windows where people were eating breakfast, washing, dressing, preparing themselves for the day. Men and women emerged with briefcases from tall gaunt houses converted into draughty flats, slammed front doors and hurried along familiar routes to catch a train or a bus. Others unlocked cars and started up engines, sometimes with difficulty due to the previous freezing night temperatures. Alan felt as if he too was part of the ordinary morning and yet he was also separate in his focus and mission. It was not every day that he was on the verge of an exciting discovery. He had not bargained for the rush-hour traffic and was feeling vulnerable on his bike. In an effort to avoid the traffic he deviated from the busy main roads and found himself following sections of the old railway that he and Rob and, lately, Marie, had discovered. Once he realised this he consciously followed the route of the old track as closely as he could. The map of the defunct Greenwich to Crystal Palace railway was firmly imprinted in his mind and images of earlier landmarks competed in his head with current ones. Crossing the traffic-choked Lewisham Way he turned off into the wide, comparatively calm Wickham Road and felt his shoulders relax slightly. It was more or less light now and the cycling was warming him up. At the church where Rob had pointed out the railway line running under the road, he glanced down at the empty track before turning right to Brockley. Children waited at bus stops, and cars edged out onto the cramped roundabout. This was the site of the old station, but it was difficult to imagine how it had all fitted in. Every so often he was parallel with a section of the railway map in his head before the road deviated temporarily, only to return to it half a mile or so later on. He cycled along streets of identical Victorian houses, threaded through a post-war council estate and past more modern flats that had been built over the track itself, then went under railway bridges and skirted cemeteries. The exhilaration of what he might be about to prove gave him extra speed. He began to fantasise headings in various art magazines:

'Antique prints dealer solves mystery location of painting.'

That made him sound old.

Or: 'Pissarro puzzle solved by print dealer in south-east London.'

Or: 'Probably Penge? Definitely not.'

He imagined himself becoming a minor celebrity in the art history circles of London and began to consider which journal he should approach for publication of such a coup.

It was completely light but still overcast by the time he reached the museum at the top of the hill. He stopped to catch his breath and take his camera out of his rucksack. He thought of Marie and how she would probably be cycling to his shop, or maybe she was already there. He could see her pedalling sedately over Deptford Creek Bridge, wrapped around with coloured scarves and woolly gloves, her beret firmly wedged over her curls, her long belted coat perilously close to the spokes of the back wheel. She was a dogged presence on the roads. He imagined with X-ray eyes the key to his shop carefully placed in the pocket of her leather satchel and knew he could depend on her and realised he increasingly wanted to. She was becoming woven into his life ever more tightly, and he was glad.

The rush-hour traffic was pretty dense by now, a mixture of lorries, buses and cars, lurching forward to the traffic lights at the bottom of the hill with the squeaking of brakes and the heady smell of exhausts. His plan was to start at the top of the hill and work his way down, taking photos of every house on the right-hand side of the road. He locked his bike to a lamppost feeling a sense of anticipation, a puzzle that had preoccupied him since his student days, niggling away in the back of his brain, surfacing every so often.

After about four shots he stopped being methodical as he saw the house at the edge of his vision. It must be the one. It stood on the corner of another road and had the three pitched roofs so clearly shown in the painting. Alan took several photos from the pavement but he was too close to fit the whole house into one shot so he had to cross the road – no easy feat in such thick traffic. Once on the other side, he leaned against the railings of an old barracks building, which was as far back as he could go. He had to pick his moment when the view was not obscured by lorries or buses. Fortunately, it was still visible over the tops of cars.

'Oh yes, this is definitely the one.' Alan spoke to himself as he took the tenth and last shot. He had to tell Marie, had to let her know she had been right and that he now had the proof. There was a phone box opposite. She would be in the shop by now. He could phone her there and tell her the good news. He felt in his pocket for the change.

SALLY

Their heads were quite close together as they looked at the photos laid out on the table. Andy had carefully put the used coffee cups on the floor and spread out the images of his paintings like a pack of cards. During break, other teachers had stopped to look at them but now the staffroom was more or less empty and Andy had the undivided attention of Sally. They discussed the locations, the composition, the brushstrokes and the colours. Sally genuinely liked them and said so. She said it was difficult to appreciate them properly on such a small scale and asked where the originals were.

'In my parents' house in Glasgow. It's one of those big old stone mansions with plenty of large chilly rooms. I was desperate to go to art college but my dad wouldn't allow it. He teaches at the university, philosophy, and thought I should continue with an academic education. What attracted me to art college, apart from the art, was the politics, the music and the feeling of that's where it was all happening. For exactly the same reasons my dad was against me going, afraid I would become a nihilist, an anarchist or both. So I was strongly encouraged to study history, which I dutifully did, but as a consolation prize my parents gave me the large dining room to use as a studio. It's pretty good, huge windows opening onto the garden, strong light, lots of space for large canvases.'

Sally sat back on her chair.

'It sounds great. I really would like to see the original paintings.'

As Andy put his photos away he leaned forward and his knee touched Sally's; neither of them moved for a minute, then Sally stood up. She wasn't sure what else she could do. Surely Andy knew she liked him. He seemed to like talking to her and was always seeking her out to discuss an exhibition or a film, but that was as far as anything went. There seemed to be an invisible fence beyond which Andy would not go.

'Can I see the pinhole camera photos?'

Sally was surprised at his interest but told him there was a display in her art room, so they left the staffroom together.

As well as the photos on the wall, Sally took out a small pile from the drawer to show him. They both laughed at the one that showed Sharon outside the school gate with what looked like a cigarette in her hand and they were still grinning at this when a head peeped round the door.

'OK if I come in?'

It was Jim, early for his lesson as usual. He joined them looking at the photos and remarked on the one of Sharon.

'She's often outside the gate smoking, usually at the far end of the playground but also at the front entrance, or at least she was the day I arrived. It didn't make too good an impression on my dad.'

Sally looked up at Jim.

'When exactly did you arrive?'

'It must have been about the third week into term. We flew into Heathrow on Sunday evening. What with jetlag and everything it was about lunchtime on Monday that my dad brought me to school for the first time.'

Andy and Sally almost spoke at the same time but Andy just got in first.

'That was the day the girl Pamela disappeared, and she was last seen at lunchtime by the school gate.'

Jim seemed quite nonchalant.

'Yes, I saw her. She was standing by the bike racks. I remember thinking I might cycle to school so I noticed her and her pink rucksack.'

'Have you told anyone about this?'

'No, well there didn't seem much point. I mean I just saw her standing there and that's all. I probably would have forgotten about it except for her photo being plastered all over the place.'

Sally spoke directly to Jim. 'I think you should go and talk to the policeman, you know the one who is investigating the case. His office is in the old geography room near the staffroom.'

'OK, but I don't have any other information.'

'Just go and see him. In fact, go now.'

Later that day, on the interminable journey home, Sally considered her work colleagues as the bus crawled in fits and starts along the South Circular. There were many young teachers, some new like her and others who had been there for a few years. This proportion of young and mainly single teachers opened up a whole new social life. One of the science teachers was a disc jockey in his spare time and had already offered to 'gig' at the staff Christmas social. So far, apart from Andy, there were no other teachers who interested Sally.

They had all been recruited for the burgeoning population of children. The school felt vibrant, chaotic, noisy and unpredictable and the pupils in it were truly a mixture of class and race. There was an unruly healthiness about so much diversity that was challenging but also refreshing. The pupils' bus journeys home, snaking lines through south London, would take them in different directions to Forest Hill, or Dulwich Village, Brixton or Peckham, to a council flat on a housing estate or a preserved Victorian villa.

As Sally's bus stopped at the space where Freddy's flat had been, she thought of him again and how he might be contacted. She still hadn't managed to track him down. In the dark of the late winter's afternoon, the area was floodlit. Sally saw a builder coming out of a small concrete building with a corrugated iron roof. As the bus moved on, she realised it must have been an air-raid shelter.

Sally considered the older members of staff. Some of them must be the same age as her parents or even her grandparents and could have seen active service in the Second World War. Did this explain her feelings of inadequacy? She had so little 'life experience' to draw on, in both her teaching and in her attempts at order in the classroom. The interview with Mr Gibson had reminded her that age and experience were no guarantee of being a good teacher. You needed to feel at ease with yourself and Sally didn't as yet, and she could tell Mr Gibson didn't either despite years of experience. Mr Booth was different though, brusque, possibly frightening to younger children, but fair and direct with their best interests at heart. Children picked up on this immediately. They knew if you were on their side, but they could also smell your fear and would play to it. Would she ever feel confident in this role as a teacher? At the moment, she felt as if a puppet stood just in front of her and went through the motions of instructions, discipline and explaining. The 'real' her was just an observer standing slightly behind, like a shadow.

The bus finally reached her stop. Sally jumped off at the top of the village, wanting to pick up some food. Soup would be good, something warming. She thought of the kitchen in the house, always gently heated at this hour by the boiler, the warmth gradually seeping around the room but cooling by the door and venturing no further into the chilly area of the hall and draughty staircase. Reg might have a saucepan boiling away on the stove. He seemed to cook unidentifiable lumps of meat very slowly for hours on end, maybe throwing in a few carrots by the afternoon. To accompany his meals he would often mix yellow powdered mustard in egg cups that would be found days later scattered around the kitchen with thick congealed skin. Checking on the stove became one of his daily tasks after 'the breakfast rush'. Once, Sally had seen something that looked like an old face-flannel throbbing in the water of Reg's saucepan and was told it was tripe. Claire had to explain exactly what that was and at Sally's expression of disbelief and disgust said it was a 'northern thing'. On that particular occasion, Reg had added onions, which did nothing to disguise the faintly rancid meat smell that hung about in the steam. Despite the cold, the vegetarians opened the windows when coming down to prepare their cauliflower cheese.

She reached the edge of the heath and the cold air blew directly into her face. Sally fleetingly thought of Jim walking his dog and his unexpected visit and piano playing. At school, nothing had changed and Jim was still the easy-going, affable and attentive student of before. She always looked forward to seeing Andy because he was good-looking and interested in many things. There was an energy and focus in him that was very attractive, an enthusiasm for life and people. Did he have an enthusiasm for her? She wasn't sure. Her list of possible boyfriends was shrinking. Jeff had settled easily into a boring job and his main leisure activity seemed to be visiting the pub. Was his prophecy at the end of the long, hot surfing summer being the end of enjoyment and freedom coming true so soon? He seemed to be moving into a phase of habits, as if he had renounced any challenges or sense of choice. In Sally's view this seemed a lazy approach to life. Josh had never really been a serious consideration, just someone good-looking she noticed around college. The reality of his hippy lifestyle was somehow dull, dreary and not really going anywhere.

There was a neutrality in being a student. You were all together in the holding pen of student life: drinking, dancing, live music and the demands of your course. Once you left, it was up to you. What would you do? What would you become? Did she really want to be a teacher? Would she ever be good enough? Her thoughts turned again to Freddy. Maybe some of her friends down in Deptford would know where he was, whether he was working and if he was still in the country. She knew he had relatives in Australia, but could he really have gone that far?

She turned onto the crescent of grass in front of the row of houses, the wind now blowing strongly from the right. From this distance, her house looked like an advent calendar with some windows lit and others dark. She reached the front step and as she searched for her key looked down and saw a group of people round the table in the kitchen. Shutting the door against the cold, she went to join them.

December

ALAN

Neither of them had wanted to go to the party, but each had thought the other one did. They could hear the music from Marie's flat as they closed the door on her balcony. Alan would much rather have stayed in and read his book with a large glass of red wine at his side, but he didn't want to appear like an old fogey to Marie. The novelty value of observing a bunch of drunken art students and unemployed layabouts (was he sounding like his dad?) was wearing thin. Also, he wanted to be up early the next day, have a leisurely breakfast with the paper, and take a brisk walk across the heath down to the antiques market in Greenwich to buy a couple of Christmas presents. This would be followed by a coffee somewhere by the river then back to Greenwich Theatre for the lunchtime jazz and a couple of pints, then off home for roast chicken. His idea of a blissful Sunday. He probably should have said something to Marie, as she had had similar misgivings about the party and also had clear ideas about what she wanted to achieve on Sunday. She was making some glove puppets for her young cousins' Christmas presents and wanted to finish them. Neither of them spoke. Marie thought Alan wanted to go to the party. He seemed to like 'shaking a leg' and enjoyed meeting new people. Alan thought Marie wanted to catch up with her art school buddies before going home for Christmas; both were wrong.

'No need to ask which flat the party is at. You could hear that bass in Rotherhithe.'

They crossed the car park and the icy wind caught them full in the face. It had been warm in Marie's flat and they wondered again why they hadn't stayed there.

The front door of the party flat was wide open, with huddles of people in coats standing on the balcony, maybe sheltering from the music, which was so loud it seemed to reverberate against Alan's chest. As they entered, it was miraculously turned down amid shouts of 'neighbours' and 'police'. As usual, the kitchen was crowded, and smelled of spices and mulled wine. There was a small amount left at the bottom of a large saucepan so Marie finished it and Alan took a glass of beer from a party can. The living room was lit by candles and the sofas were covered with chenille curtains, probably bought from Deptford Market. They were shiny and provided rich shades of turquoise and rusty red. Every available space was filled with cushions. Now that the music had been turned down, people were returning, and it was a welcoming place to be. As usual, Alan knew nobody and sat rather uncomfortably on an ethnic patterned floor cushion. He was next to a young woman in an Afghan coat which, maybe because it was damp, smelled rather definitely of animal. He sipped his beer and looked about with an amiable expression, trying to give the impression he was at ease and relaxed, although he wasn't.

Marie had been talking to a woman with bright red hair but had momentarily left the room. Alan was relieved the music had been changed to something more melodic. He couldn't really listen to more than one track of that echoey sort of reggae without developing a headache. The young woman in the smelly coat had closed her eyes and was probably asleep, with her head slumped against Alan's arm. He could have done with another beer but it seemed difficult to move so he just sat tight and thought of all the pleasant things he wanted to do the next day, and how all the things were made more enjoyable by doing them with Marie. At that moment she came back into the room, followed by a tall dark man wearing a double-breasted pin-striped suit. It was the sort of suit his father might have worn twenty years ago, and if Alan had worn such a thing he would have looked like a middle-aged stockbroker, but on this thin young man it looked razor sharp and surprisingly modern. They were talking and laughing at some shared joke, and from his vantage point Alan thought how good they looked together, Marie in her black crushed velvet dress with a bronze belt, and this young man with short greased hair and navy pin-stripes, a glimpse of braces as the jacket swung open.

They could have been in a film about the Second World War. Marie smiled across at him but continued to talk to the slim man who only had eyes for her and was standing very close.

The sleeping woman in the smelly coat woke up and asked Alan where the toilet was. He wasn't sure, but helped her up and into the corridor. She only just made it before throwing up. As Alan pushed past the clumps of people on his way back to the living room he wondered what on earth he was doing at this party, and thought how he would rather be at home. He would ask Marie if they could leave. His first sight on entering the candlelit room was Marie in the arms of the thin suited man, dancing to a slow Otis Redding track. It all looked very cosy. Before he had time to think, Alan strode across the room and tapped Marie on the arm, saying 'Can I have a word?'

The man had his back to Alan, and Marie's head was resting on his shoulder. She mouthed 'In a minute'.

Alan was irritated and went outside to stand on the balcony. Marie joined him a few minutes later. She linked her arm through his and asked him if he was all right. Alan pulled his arm away roughly.

'No, not really. I would like to go home. I didn't want to come in the first place but I don't want to break up your intimate little assignation.' Why did his vocabulary become like a crossword clue when he was angry?

'Oh, Alan don't be silly. I was just dancing with Rupert. He was in my painting group and left the course

228

to manage a band so I haven't seen him for over a year. He's just an old friend. I was going to introduce you but you didn't give me a chance.'

It all sounded perfectly reasonable but Alan was in no mood for understanding.

'I'm going home. Don't let me cramp your style.'

'Come on, Alan, stop this. There's nothing to be angry about.'

'Isn't there?'

'No, not at all. Come back inside. It's cold out here.'

Marie was shivering and her shoulders were shaking. Alan glimpsed the thin suit watching them from the kitchen window, and the sight of him fuelled his temper. Part of him wanted to gather her in his arms, stop the shaking and warm her up, but the other half was still angry.

'Sod this, I'm off.'

He turned and walked towards the stairwell.

Marie shouted after him.

'I thought I was staying at yours tonight.'

'Stay and talk to your friend.'

He was down on the forecourt and across the other side of the car park before he looked back. There was no one on the balcony now and the door to the party had been shut. He had the long walk home to regret his behaviour. What was wrong with him? He was acting like a jealous teenager. Marie must wonder what had got into him. He wondered that himself. Not for the first time he asked himself what she saw in him. She was an attractive young art student with lots of interesting friends. He was a collector of antique prints and maps, obsessed by an old railway line. When they were out together he felt self-conscious in his traditional clothes, and wondered if he appeared like an uncle or older brother. He had only really had one serious girlfriend and Marie had been out with several of the art students. He felt inexperienced, old and boring.

As he passed the single-storey wooden building that had been the railway station at the bottom of Blackheath Hill, he considered going back to Marie's flat to apologise, but he was scared. Maybe the thin suit would be there, invited back for coffee.

As he reached the summit of the hill, the cold wind from the exposed heath hit him and he was glad to arrive at his own front door. Once inside, he sat by the gas fire with his coat on and sipped a glass of brandy. He wanted to phone Marie. He wanted to speak to her, but she didn't have a phone in her flat. He would have to wait until the morning. He ran a hot bath and took the bottle into the steamy room. Lying in the suds, he regretted his stupid behaviour and determined to make it up to Marie as soon as he could. He put an extra blanket on the bed as there was no warmth from another body, and after he had wedged a newspaper under the window to stop the rattling from the north-east wind, he finally fell asleep.

The ringing of his phone woke him and he stumbled out into the hallway, still wearing thick socks and a jumper over his pyjamas. His first thought was that it must be Marie, and he felt let down when he heard Rob's voice.

'Alan, hallo. I'm in a flat in Chelsea.'

'Oh, what are you doing there?'

'It doesn't matter. The point is. I'm looking at the November edition of *Art Collector* magazine and there's a bloody big article on Pissarro and his London paintings and, what's more, a special feature confirming the location of the railway station previously thought to be Penge.'

'Lordship Lane?'

'Yup, the very same. I'm sorry, mate, but it looks like you've been pipped to the post on this one. There are photos of past and present views, all backing up the validity of the locations. The one of the railway station shows a steam train heading for the bridge that's in those woods. I think the photo was taken in the early fifties.'

Alan was back with his father on the same bridge, anxious about his new school and with a half-crown in his coat pocket.

'Christ, I can't believe it.'

'Yeah, it's bloody hard luck, bad timing. I'm sorry to be the bearer of bad news old man, but I thought you should know as soon as possible.'

'Yes, I appreciate you telling me. What are you doing in Chelsea?'

'Just visiting someone. Anyway, I'll "borrow" this copy of the mag to show you the article. It won't be missed here. Will you be around for a lunchtime pint?'

After Alan put the phone down, he went into the kitchen to make some tea. He boiled the kettle, spooned the leaves into the teapot and put some milk in his cup before allowing himself to consider what Rob had just told him. He took the tea back to bed, the warmest place in the flat, and mulled over the facts. If the article was in the November issue of the magazine, it would have been submitted in October at the latest and the writer must have known the location of the railway painting before that, whereas he had only been fully certain for a few days. Nevertheless, the news was a blow, as he had been truly excited at having discovered something, but now it seemed someone else had got there before him.

Inevitably his thoughts turned to Marie, who had been an integral part of the process in the last couple of months, organising the information and photos into the sketchbooks, and being so enthusiastically involved. She was always ready to discuss possibilities and spend time on research. Most importantly, it was her suggestion that the houses in the background of the painting could confirm the location, and she'd been right.

Alan shuffled back to the kitchen and, feeling rather sorry for himself, poured a second cup of tea. He felt terrible about the night before, embarrassed and ashamed of his childish behaviour with Marie, and also disappointed and deflated by Rob's news. He wondered whether he should discontinue the railway project. The fact that someone else had confirmed the location of the Pissarro painting had knocked the wind out of his sails. Was it worth visiting the last two stations? What was the point of it all now?

Suddenly he knew what he had to do. He started getting dressed, just putting on the clothes nearest to hand. If he didn't go now he might never go at all. He had to visit the last two stations just to see the project through and there was no time like the present. Alan unlocked the bike shed and as he wheeled his bike onto the heath he remembered his camera, so he shot back into the flat. Ten minutes later on a cold, grey Sunday morning, he was pedalling fast in the direction of Crystal Palace.

WILSON

It had become a sort of routine. Valerie Jones and Ray Wilson would meet every Friday evening after work in the pub at the end of the road. Originally, they had met to discuss the case of the missing girl and they still did chew over the latest facts or lack of them, but increasingly they talked about more personal things. Ray found it easy to talk to Val. She asked direct questions but didn't appear to pry or get too personal as many women did. Consequently, he found himself telling her about his wife and children and even his hopes and dreams for the future. As a policeman, Ray could retire with a decent pension at fifty and, as he was only a few years away from this age, he had begun to consider his options. He wanted to be near the sea, to buy a boat and be out in the fresh air. He fancied the Suffolk coast where he holidayed whenever he could, keeping an eye on the ever-changing sky and enjoying the decent fish and chips and friendly pubs. He liked talking to the fishermen and knew once he had a boat he could be part of their group, not fishing commercially, but going out every so often, fixing his nets and messing about on the shingle. In London, particularly the south-east, he would be forever wary, wondering if someone would recognise him as the copper who had 'banged up our brother'. He would always be looking over his shoulder, both physically and metaphorically. It would not be easy to relax. Out on the Suffolk coast, where the crime rate was low, he would be free from his dealings as a policeman.

Ray attributed his interest in the sea to his grandfather, who had been a lighterman on the River Thames and taken goods from the Port of London up to Harwich. Once, as a small boy, Ray had been allowed to accompany him, and the experience was imprinted in his mind. He remembered the early start in the dark, the slithering ropes and the chug of the engine starting and the absolute cold of his hands wrapped around a hot mug of tea with three sugars. Then the boat was heading out through dark waters towards the sea. Gradually, the river opened out and it became light. Ray had felt he was on a voyage, a unique and special journey like something from one of his *Adventure Annuals for Boys*.

Ray considered his grandfather had done something worthwhile and important. Taking goods from the docks to Harwich was very tangible to a boy, and far more understandably useful than working in an office, as his father had done. As Ray played with his toy lorries, he was always driving to the London docks or the Port at Harwich, never to his father's office in Croydon.

Valerie also spoke about her family. Coming from Nottingham, her grandfather had worked in the mines. She barely remembered him as he had died of lung cancer when she was five years old. There was a vague recollection of sitting on his knee one Christmas and rough hands helping her untie a ribbon on a present. Her own father had worked as a foreman in a local factory, not wanting to follow the dangerous dirty life in the pits.

Both Val and Ray felt they had bettered themselves and moved their families up a notch, gaining a small distance along the road away from manual labour. And yet it was their grandfathers they both admired and respected more than their own fathers.

After their second drink, Ray turned the conversation back to the school and asked Val about Mr Gibson.

'What's he like, this Gibson?'

'A bit weak, well-meaning but ineffectual. I think he got his head of house post when the school opened and has just sort of stayed on. He's the type that thinks his position should command respect rather than earning it for himself. Some of the female staff think he's a bit creepy and I don't think he knows how to talk to them as work colleagues. He feels nervous, so he tries to be charming in a silly old-fashioned sort of way that gets misconstrued.'

'I've only interviewed him twice but he strikes me as incompetent.'

Valerie emptied her glass. 'To be fair, he hasn't been well recently. In fact, he was in hospital for the first few weeks of term.'

Wilson shook his head and sighed.

'It seems difficult to get rid of ineffective teachers. I've seen a few in the last couple of months that shouldn't be in charge of a class. I mean, if you're no good at your job, you should get the sack. That's what happens in the real world.'

Valerie bristled at the implication that teaching was not the real world. She thought of all the difficult families she had encountered, the social workers she had liaised with, and the sad, confused children she saw every day. They all lived in the real world and had real problems.

'I don't suppose any profession is immune from weaker members, even the police, is it?'

Ray smiled. 'You're right. One for the road?'

ALAN

Alan took the route that was now familiar to him, following the track of the old railway line, almost. The roads were fairly empty. A few people were popping out for Sunday papers then hurrying home to get back into the warm. There was a deserted feel in the streets, partly due to the fact that it was the weekend and partly because of the cold. Despite his gloves, Alan's fingers were frozen and he was glad he'd worn Rob's old beret. As he cycled, snatches of his argument with Marie the previous evening came into his head. Had he really said 'Don't let me cramp your style'?

He shuddered at this and then the memory of walking off in a huff. Such stupid behaviour. These thoughts were mixed in with the aim of his journey, visiting the last two stations on the Crystal Palace railway. He had read countless times that the line had never really been successful since its opening in 1862. He knew that the number of passengers using it remained low due to the catchment area that included cemeteries, waterworks and low density Victorian villa development.

Alan was now cycling through the disappointing catchment area which, over a hundred years later, was still sparsely populated though with concentrated clusters of new housing. The Victorian villas were still there, some converted into flats, others with new apartment blocks squeezed into their once generous gardens. The leafiness remained, along with the sense of secrecy. London as a city might have expanded on the edges, spread relentlessly into the suburbs, but pockets nearer the centre retained their original scale and layout. The once separate villages kept a kernel of character, evident in a row of shops, the width of a street or an old tree outside a pub. Presumably this is why house prices were increasing in such areas. People could pretend. They could carry their baskets to the local grocer and buy a few choice items before driving to the local supermarket to stock up on washing powder and cornflakes. They enjoyed browsing in the second-hand bookshop and drinking the freshly brewed coffee in the local café. They had the best of both worlds, but they had to pay for it.

Alan thought again of the man in the suit, whom he pictured with his arms around Marie's waist. Then, the image of the two of them dancing so close and Marie looking at Alan over his shoulder had been the worst moment, the one when his jealousy had really kicked in. Once he'd taken these photos he would cycle over to her flat and apologise. Hopefully, he would find her alone.

Alan arrived at Upper Sydenham, the penultimate station on the old Crystal Palace line and stopped outside the booking office and station house, now privately owned. He had many old photos of this well-documented station and didn't feel the need to take many of his own. He knew the line would have passed behind and below the building in front of him and continued into the first tunnel just visible, though boarded up and lost in the grass. It was strange the way in just twenty years or so the land had risen up, or was the tunnel sinking? Maybe the council had shifted earth or rubble here to flatten the land that was now mainly used by dog walkers. He couldn't see the second tunnel, which was hidden in the woods further on and would take the train all the way to the plateau of what was Crystal Palace high-level station. That was now his aim and he turned his bike in that direction.

Despite the disappointing news from Rob about the magazine article, Alan was still excited about this final visit. The station, once the grandest and largest of them all, was long gone. The final destination, built in red brick, two square towers at each corner and four tracks wide, was a fitting introduction to the scale and importance of the Crystal Palace itself. Alan's main interest was a subway under the Parade that had linked the Crystal Palace directly with the station. He had seen photos of a wide vaulted and tiled chamber resembling a Byzantine crypt with beautiful terracotta and cream bricks. He knew the tunnel had been designed and built by cathedral craftsmen brought over from Italy. He also knew that the entrance had been well and truly secured, a reflection of how seriously the council intended to keep out intruders. The underground walkway was a listed building and needed to be vandal proof. Alan had been reading some back copies of *Railway World* when he realised there might be a way in. The article reminded him that the line had been electrified in the 1920s, and this had involved building a sub-station and a shaft to provide the power cable connection. Alan had worked out where this shaft might be and was planning to use it as access.

The petrol station seemed a good place to park his bike, as he wanted some distance between what he was about to do and any evidence of his presence. This spot had also been the site of a Pissarro painting 'The Crystal Palace'. He took a crumpled postcard of it out of his jacket. In the painting, the sun was shining on what appeared to be a Sunday as families wandered along the Parade with the Palace on the left. A flag on a pole was blowing in what looked like a warm breeze. The road and paths were a soft, sandy colour and the sky a light turquoise. Several Victorian villas stood behind wooden fences and gates on the right of the painting. The whole scene looked calm and inviting.

Alan put the postcard of the painting back in his pocket. He stood in more or less the same spot that Pissarro must have painted from. The scene he looked at was very different: no palace, and just a television tower in place of the flagpole; no Victorian villas, just a petrol station. But most noticeable was the lack of people and the lack of any reason for people to be there. There was just a stretch of road leading from the traffic lights to the small roundabout where the buses waited.

What had been an attractive parade with an impressive building was now an ugly stretch of road with the sense of a large gap.

He walked almost the full length of the Parade then took the steps that led down to where the old Crystal Palace station platforms would have been. Now it was just nondescript scrubland with a few dumped fridges and a burned-out caravan among other unidentifiable rubbish. About a hundred yards away were the remaining prefabs that had not yet been pulled down. Level with the third step was the cover to the shaft. Alan was relieved that it was slightly lower than the pavement and behind a wall so that he would not be entirely visible from the road. He could be seen from the prefabs but they looked more or less unoccupied. He had come prepared with a chisel and a trowel in case he had to dig or prise the cover open, but in the end he didn't need anything. Suprisingly, the cover was quite loose and seemed to have been used recently. Inside, a metal ladder descended to a lower tunnel that was about four feet high, so Alan had to bend as he made his way towards the underground walkway. Reaching it, he straightened up, his back aching momentarily as he stood stretching and adjusting his eyes to the dimly lit surroundings. Whoever had secured the outside entrance had left a strong mesh strip at the top, letting in both pale light and air. Even without his torch he could make out the curving structures of the octagonal pillars and appreciate the warm pink and cream of the brickwork.

'Beautiful,' he said to himself, and then shone his torch upwards to see the top of the pillars more clearly. As his torch explored around the space, Alan reminded himself that thousands of people would have thronged through this walkway, pushing their way from the train to the Great Exhibition. Subsequent crowds would have passed this way, at different times of the day throughout the weeks and years, gradually thinning out until 1954 when the station closed. It had stood derelict until being demolished in 1961. In his mind's eye he visualised a speeded-up film with men and women in different decades of costume crossing and re-crossing this space with parasols, top hats, bustles and bowlers. Gloves would have been dropped, toffee papers thrown down, newspapers trampled underfoot, railway tickets chucked into corners. Yet the architecture was that of a church. It was certainly a grand start to visiting the Palace that would have been the destination on the other side.

Alan zigzagged his torch downwards from the ceiling to a floor of grey and black tiles in some sort of pattern that was unclear in such gloomy light. He took his camera out, adjusted the flash and attached the zoom lens. Looking through the viewfinder, he focused at ground level, and on this larger scale noticed a pile of coal and rags in the far corner. He walked across to get a better look. Looking down he saw what looked like an anorak. For an instant he was reminded of the stuffed guys that were made by children on the fifth of November. It occurred to him that he should bend down to investigate further, but despite the freezing cold an unpleasant smell hit him. He turned away in disgust but knew he had to confirm his suspicions. It might be easier to use the camera. He stepped back and wound his scarf over his nose and mouth to block the smell then focused the lens towards what was still recognisable as a face. He took several shots partly to confirm what he was seeing and also as proof and evidence. The overwhelming desire to get out of that space, away from this awful discovery and to tell someone made his hands shake, but he managed five shots. A feeling of nausea overwhelmed him and he turned to go. Fumbling to put his camera in his bag, he tripped and, looking down among the rubbish, saw the strap of a pink rucksack wound around his shoe.

SALLY

Sally held the pile of papers in her hand on top of the register. The tutor group were quiet and subdued. They knew what was coming, had seen the news on television, overheard teachers and parents discussing it in urgent tones. The photo of Pamela Webb was burned into their brains, Pamela Webb who had been missing for over three months but who had now been found, dead. Pamela, who had been one of them, had worn their uniform and walked their streets. Their school was now famous, in the spotlight by association. Cousins and distant friends phoned; did they know the girl? Had they any idea who had done it? Was there anyone suspicious at the school?

Sally told everyone to sit down and take out a pen. The police had issued a list of questions they wanted each child in the school to answer. The usual fuss of pupils asking to borrow pens or dropping pencils on the floor didn't happen. This dramatic incident had taken place in their area, the victim was one of them and they were numbed into silence, taking this seriously. Sally went through all the questions to check everybody understood. At the top of the sheet of paper was an underlined heading:

Re: Missing Child – Pamela WEBB now dead.
As you know, the body of Pamela Webb was found last weekend under the railway arch at the site of the old Crystal Palace Railway Station which is situated on Crystal Palace Parade near the junction with Farquhar Road, sketch map attached.
Pamela was last seen at about 1pm on Monday 25th September at the school gates. We would like to trace anyone who:
1   Saw her after this time. There are several buses that leave from the Crystal Palace Parade, which is just across the road.

2   Saw her. If so, did they notice whether she was carrying anything, i.e. a rucksack containing school books?
3   Has accompanied or seen Pamela at the railway arches on Crystal Palace Parade.
4   Frequents the waste ground near the railway arches or knows of any other person who does.
5   Knows of any reason why Pamela Webb might have gone to the waste ground.
6   Saw anyone suspicious in the vicinity of the waste ground, particularly on, or immediately after, 25th September.
7   Has been on the waste ground since 25th September.

Should any person have such information, please contact the police.

While the children wrote, Sally felt the light in the room was changing and looking out she saw it was snowing. Light, thin flakes blew about, but were also settling on the grey tarmac of the courtyard like powder, creating an effect of softening that was to Sally's eyes slightly sinister in the sense that things were covered so you were not entirely sure what they were. Some of the children looked up too and saw the snow, excitement registering on their faces.

No one could really help with the murder inquiry. Elaine had caught a bus from the Parade that day but couldn't remember seeing anything out of the ordinary.

Lisa had a friend whose dad was a bus driver. He might have stopped there on that day. Karen's mum worked in a shop nearby just off the roundabout.

'OK, everyone, thank you for your help. Just leave your sheets of paper on the front desk and go quietly to break.'

Several children spoke to her on the way out.

'Do they have any suspects, Miss?'

'Will they get who did it?'

'Will they hang them?'

Sally smoothed over their questions and ushered them from the room. She knew nothing more than they did.

Twenty minutes later, after a quick cup of coffee in the staffroom, she stepped out into the playground, now covered in snow, and relished the silence, both the absence of classroom noise and the softness of the muffled outside. Walking towards the gate, she breathed deeply the cold air and enjoyed the feeling of being alone and having escaped. This was truly a free period. The snow was falling thickly now, settling on the gate and in between the school railings, forming a white line on the black. There was no other person in sight as she slipped out from the school, crunching across the new snow on her way to the bank. With each step she distanced herself from all the current teaching concerns, her lesson plans, registers, detentions, naughty children and, of course, the fact that Pamela Webb's body had now been found.

Sally walked lightly along the pavement, her footsteps the first impressions in the new snow. She passed the bridge and the pub at the end of the road and turned left towards the cluster of shops; a greengrocer, a stationery shop, a wool shop, a small supermarket and the bank. She had been here a few times, to this dowdy now forgotten backwater. The stationer's had pads of paper and envelopes arranged in boxes on the floor looking as though the owner might suddenly have to leave and take his stock with him. The greengrocer sometimes had a bit of fruit and veg displayed on the pavement – muddy potatoes, a few cabbages and wrinkly apples. Today there was nothing outside, just small drifts of snow against the empty boxes, the door firmly shut. The stationer's looked closed, as if the shopkeeper hadn't bothered to get out of bed.

Strangely, the bank was quite crowded and the floor was wet with melted snow from boots. Sally took her place in the queue and recognised the policeman, Detective Inspector Wilson, standing two people in front of her. Just seeing him made her feel slightly guilty. He had interviewed her a few weeks ago and she had been quite worried that he would ask to see her class registers for the day that Pamela had disappeared. If he had, he would have seen a gap on that particular Monday. In fact, he'd only wanted to discuss the pinhole camera photos and she showed him the small number of clear images she had. He had asked a few questions about Sharon and Nick, and after a few minutes had said she could go.

Sally had been surprised and relieved at the brevity of the interview, but still every time she saw him she couldn't shake off the feeling that she was slightly in the wrong.

ROB

Rob knew where the estate was but had never visited anyone there before. He sat in his father's car, borrowed the day before, in a traffic jam that seemed to stretch all the way from the heath down to New Cross and beyond. For all he knew it could be chock-a-block all the way to the Elephant and Castle. It was a damp, slightly foggy morning and very cold. A dusting of snow had settled on the kerbs. He had been at a standstill for at least five minutes and was glad of the heater blasting hot air onto his feet.

When he had first met Marie, Rob had considered her an unlikely match for Alan and didn't think it would last. At that first meeting, Marie was dressed as though she worked on a building site and had been quite curt in answering his questions. He had remarked later to Alison that she had verged on being rude. The second time, the four of them had met in a pub, and Rob had been surprised at how different Marie looked, plump and pretty in a velvet dress and fur coat. On that occasion, she had been good fun and had even teased him, which Alison found very amusing. Marie had been openly affectionate to Alan, stroking his arm and kissing him as they stood together at the bar.

'Who would have thought it?' Alison remarked as they watched Alan and Marie order more drinks. 'I'm so pleased for Alan. They look very happy together. He deserves someone good for a change after the histrionics of Fiona.'

Rob had to agree. Alan deserved a bit of luck.

'She's also one of our best watercolourists. Her prints always sell.'

Rob changed gear and moved forward about ten feet, but the traffic lights turned red just as he reached them. He sighed and looked again at his watch. Fifteen minutes later he turned into the car park of Marie's flat. He found the whole area depressing, with rubbish spilling out of the chutes and dodgy-looking cars jacked up with no wheels, and reflected that it was not somewhere he would choose to live. He understood the attraction of low rent but it was all too grim for him. Although the students and social workers were starting to outnumber the original tenants, there was even now an uneasy animosity. To Rob, the smell of violence and poverty still clung to the dirty bricks and there was an air of menace about the whole place. Not for the first time he felt grateful for his father's contribution towards his own rent, which enabled him to live in his spacious Victorian flat on the edge of the heath – draughty and expensive, but definitely in the right area.

Rob locked the car and looked along the balconies, working out that Marie must be on the second floor. He didn't fancy the lift and took the stairs two at a time, arriving slightly breathless at a bright yellow door.

Marie opened the door in a thick fluffy dressing gown. She looked both sleepy and surprised.

'Rob, how did you know where I live? Come in, it's freezing.'

She shut the door.

'What is it? Has something happened to Alan?'

'Yes. He's been arrested and I've come to take you to the police station.'

MISS LLOYD

Miss Lloyd was most apologetic. She couldn't understand how such an important document had gone missing. She had put it in the file herself, so someone must have taken it out and not replaced it. Could it have been Mr Gibson, the housemaster? Surely he wouldn't have been so careless? But he had been in hospital and so the document had been on his desk for weeks and missing from the file. DI Wilson had never seen it and was not aware of the previous conviction.

Wilson drummed his fingers on the piece of paper in irritation.

'I need to speak to him urgently.'

'Yes, I thought you would, so I went to fetch him but unfortunately he's absent today.'

Miss Lloyd felt tense. Although this was strictly speaking not directly her fault, as deputy head she felt in some way responsible. Her cheeks were pink and she rubbed the skin around her fingernails in agitation. How inefficient, how incompetent. What was Mr Gibson thinking of?

Wilson stood up and put the piece of paper back into the file.

'This can't wait. I'll have to go round to his house. Is there anyone in the school who could accompany me?'

Valerie Jones had seemed the obvious choice.

When they had left, Miss Lloyd took herself off to the little-used ladies' staffroom. It was small and north-facing with a few comfortable chairs and a single bed along one wall. The younger women staff shunned it, preferring to be in the more modern cut and thrust of male and female company. The men's staffroom, which in latter years had become a sort of pipe-smoking club, had already been converted into a quiet marking room. Miss Lloyd feared their staffroom was also doomed due to lack of use, though today it provided the calm retreat she needed. She sighed as she sank into one of the armchairs. Twenty years ago, when the school opened, a bed had been installed in here at her suggestion. She had become accustomed to this at her previous post at a girls' high school, where it proved useful at certain times of the month. Maybe young women these days took painkillers or were on the pill so they didn't suffer so much; at any rate, what she had thought of as a civilised gesture was hardly used and had become a bit of a white elephant. Miss Lloyd took off her glasses and cleaned them with a handkerchief. The discovery of poor Pamela Webb's body was disturbing enough, but now the possibility of there being a killer among the pupils was even more distressing.

Already the school had been inundated with phone calls from the press, and the office staff had been instructed not to speak to anyone. There would be a police statement as soon as anything definite was known, but meanwhile nothing would be said.

Miss Lloyd leaned against the back of the chair and closed her eyes. She had dealt several times with the death of children in her long teaching career, a few of these during the war. Her school at that time was in Plumstead and had been close to the Woolwich Arsenal where many houses had suffered direct hits. She remembered a particular couple, distraught parents, who had come to inform her of the death of their daughter during a night raid. Having listened to their story she had unexpectedly broken down. Normally so composed and calm, she had given in to shaking sobs. The parents ended up comforting her, without realising she had that morning received a telegram informing her of the death of Anthony, her fiancé, killed in action somewhere in North Africa. She had never married.

Since that time there had been a list of children who had died in different circumstances: knocked off their bikes, killed in car crashes or by contracting fatal illnesses, but in over forty years of teaching Miss Lloyd had never had to deal with a murder. It was now confirmed that Pamela Webb had been strangled and her body had lain there in the tunnel under the road for almost three months. Miss Lloyd shivered and pulled her cardigan tighter. The room was slightly chilly and the small radiator inadequate. Well, she couldn't sit here all day. 'There are things to do. There are always things to do,' she murmured to herself. There was a never-ending list of people to see, paperwork to go through, phone calls to make. The catalogue of tasks spilled over into her weekends and evenings. Her work flooded her life. She had allowed it to and, in some ways, she welcomed it.

WILSON

Wilson and Valerie Jones parked outside Carson House, an older four-storey block of flats, and carried on the conversation they had started in the car. Wilson put his overcoat on.

'I just want to get this straight. As housemaster, Mr Gibson had the file and nobody else in the school knew about the previous incident?'

The wind was whipping thin strands of Valerie's hair into her mouth, and she tried unsuccessfully to extricate them.

'Miss Lloyd, the Head, and Mr Gibson as housemaster would definitely have known. I think most of the staff were aware of what happened last year. It would have been assumed all the documentation, all the information surrounding the events, would have been in the file and therefore you would have been aware of the previous incident yourself.'

'It wasn't though. Did you not think to tell me?'

'I really thought you already knew, that you must have known.'

'So, Gibson failed to return the documentation to the file. It's been sitting in his office muddled up in a heap of papers.'

'Yes, it seems so and then he was in hospital.'

'Exactly. More time wasted. Whichever way you look at it, he's been bloody incompetent. I don't believe it. Such important evidence hidden for so long.'

The flat was at the end of the third-floor balcony, a frozen coconut mat and two empty milk bottles the only sign of habitation. A smartly dressed woman answered their knock and visibly tensed at the word 'police'.

'Come in. You're lucky you caught me, I was just off to work. Nick is at home today. Not feeling too good, so I thought it best he stays in the warm. He wasn't at school yesterday either. Must be a touch of flu.'

They followed her clicking heels into a tidy living room where there was a large red sofa, a small TV, a sideboard and matching coffee table. Nick was sitting in an armchair by the window. He looked up and smiled. A small notebook and biro slid to the floor as he stood up.

'Mrs Powell, we need to take Nick down to the police station for questioning and would be grateful if you could accompany us. We have a few questions about the missing girl Pamela Webb.'

Nick's mother seemed confused and momentarily lost for words. She looked at Wilson and across to her son as if she might find an explanation of this strange turn of events in either of their expressions. Both faces were blank, though Nick appeared alert, almost expectant and was still smiling slightly. Mrs Powell seemed to rouse herself into action as indicated by the slight shake of the ruffles on her blouse. She turned and looked directly at Wilson.

'Should I phone my work, tell them I won't be in, only I was just leaving and they'll be expecting me.'

'Yes, that would be a good idea.'

Her heels clicked out of the room and left a silence. Wilson looked at his notes, Nick looked out of the window and Valerie Jones looked at Nick. Mrs Powell returned a few minutes later holding her coat.

'You'd better tell me what this is all about. Is Nick in trouble again?' She looked accusingly at Wilson as if he himself could be the cause of any trouble just by being there and by being a policeman.

'We don't know anything for certain. We just need to ask Nick a few questions down at the station. Hopefully he can help us.'

It didn't take long to drive through the empty streets. There were slabs of dirty snow not quite melted at the edges of the pavements and a few people stood at bus stops.

The police station, not far from the roundabout near the school, was new territory for Valerie. Their small group trooped past the reception desk and walked in single file down the endless tiled corridors. A policewoman with a tape recorder joined them in the interview room.

Wilson sat at a desk and motioned for Nick to sit opposite.

'Ask me then.'

Nick's voice was strangely authoritative and there was a change in his expression that Valerie couldn't quite read.

Wilson looked directly at him.

'Where were you on the afternoon that Pamela Webb disappeared?'

'At school.'

'Are you sure? You weren't in lessons. You were marked absent for both English and geography.'

'It could have been the dentist. Nick's had quite a bit of trouble with his teeth recently, haven't you, Nick?'

'Mrs Powell, I would be grateful if you could let Nick answer for himself.'

It had started to rain again, grey balls of sleet hitting the window and adding to the general gloomy light. Nick looked at the floor.

Wilson tried again.

'So, Nick, where were you on that afternoon?'

'It could have been one of my probation appointments, changed from a Tuesday.'

'I have already checked with your probation officer. All your appointments since the summer have been on a Tuesday afternoon. We are talking about a Monday afternoon in the first few weeks of term, only a few months ago. If you were bunking off, you would remember.'

Mrs Powell couldn't help herself.

'What about them apples? You came home with a bag full, said you'd been scrumping at the vicarage. Was it that Monday?'

Nick just shook his head and looked out of the window.

Wilson tried another tack.

'Nick, when I interviewed you at the school you said you knew Pamela. Can you tell us again how well you knew her? Were you a friend of hers?'

'Like I said before, I did know her a bit. I spoke to her on the first day at the bus stop. Some stupid second-year boys were fighting in the queue, trying to act big, and I could see she, Pamela, was a bit scared but trying not to show it. She was on her own. So I threatened them, said I'd report them. I protected her.

Since then I think she had a sort of crush on me, you know like young girls do.'

Mrs Powell interrupted again.

'That was decent of you Nicky, wasn't it, Inspector?'

Wilson nodded in her direction and carried on.

'Did you speak to her after that first day?'

'Once or twice. I told her if she had any trouble with anyone to come and see me and I would sort it out. I liked her. She was sort of a loner but strong. She did have friends but she wasn't always hanging around with bunches of silly giggling girls.'

'Did you see her outside school?'

'Yeah, I said, at the bus stop.'

'On any other occasion?'

'I don't think so.'

Mrs Powell stood up, obviously nervous and unable to stop herself fidgeting.

She sat down again and fumbled in her handbag for a packet of cigarettes, which she took out, lighting a slightly crumpled one. Her hands shook slightly as she narrowed her eyes against the smoke and crossed and re-crossed her legs.

Wilson was circling, trying to find a way in. He started from another direction.

'Nick, did you know a man called Stanley Riley?'

'If you mean Stan the old gypo who lived in the caravan, then, yes, I knew him a bit.'

'Did you visit him in his caravan?'

'A few times, in the summer, I went up there, took some bones for his dog, got chatting. He was all right. He'd certainly lived a life.'

'When you went to see him, did you go alone?'

'Yes.'

'Always?'

'Yes. I got friendly with his dog and he knew he could trust me. I wasn't scared like most kids. Stan was good to talk to, told me stories, how he'd survived on his wits, lived rough in the old station. Sometimes I took him food.'

'Did you talk to anyone else about Stan?'

'Maybe Sharon. I might have mentioned him to her.'

'What about Pamela Webb.'

'I don't think so. I didn't know her very well.'

'So, you didn't ever talk to Pamela Webb about Stan Riley?'

'I might have done. I can't remember.'

At almost the same time, Wilson and Valerie Jones realised where Nick might be leading them and how at this point he might need to backtrack. Sure enough, he reviewed his story.

'Yes, I think I did talk to her about Stan. She was interested that he lived in a caravan, said she'd like to see it.'

'So did you offer to take her?'

'I think I said we could go on a Saturday but we never got round to it before she, you know, disappeared.'

'So do you think she could have gone on her own?

Did she know exactly where it was? Did she know how to get there by herself?

Nick appeared to be thinking about his answers to these questions. His fists were clenched and he looked down at the scuffed floor.

'Yes, she could.'

'But is it likely, Nick? A young girl, new to the school, just taking off on a Monday afternoon to see an old man in a caravan? Why would she do that?'

'I did mention the puppies.'

'What puppies?'

'Well, Stan's dog had had three puppies and he wanted to give them away, get rid of them, as he couldn't cope with his own dog, let alone puppies.'

Valerie Jones looked up. The room felt oppressive and she was developing a headache.

Wilson leaned further forward in his chair, his eyes fixed intently on Nick, who met his gaze then looked away. Wilson spoke in a slightly quieter voice.

'Nick, did you go with Pamela Webb on that Monday afternoon to see Stanley with the promise she could have a free puppy?'

'No.'

'Do you think she went on her own to see Stanley to get a puppy?'

'She might have done. I told her he would drown them if no one wanted them, so she might have gone by herself. She must have done, 'cos that's where the body was found, wasn't it?'

Nick was talking loudly now, his calm manner lost. Breathing loudly through his nose he continued.

'I mean she could have gone there to get a puppy and old Stanley got confused and went for her.'

'Went for her?'

'Yes, you know, hit her or something. He didn't like kids. That's why he had the Alsatian. I mean something like that must have happened. The body was found close to his caravan, wasn't it? He was a mad old man – he could have done anything. Maybe he didn't even realise what he was doing, maybe he didn't mean to strangle her. Maybe he was even sorry when he realised what he had done but it was too late so he hid the body in the tunnel.'

Nick was aware that he had said too much. He had meant to stick to answering questions in the briefest way but now he had gone on too long and given them the whole story. He had given them the story he wanted them to gradually deduce for themselves. Too late.

Valerie Jones sat with tense hunched shoulders. She sensed they were getting somewhere at last, and her head throbbed.

Wilson spoke again to Nick.

'Nick, how do you think an old man like Stanley could have got into the tunnel that led to the underground space where Pamela was found, assuming he even knew it was there? It would be extremely difficult to lug a body all that way even for a young man, let alone an old one like Stanley who was not in the best of health.'

There was another silence, as if Wilson wanted the information to sink in. He continued 'I think you did go with Pamela to see Stanley on that Monday afternoon, and you put pressure on her by telling her the puppies would be killed if she didn't go. You met her by the school gate. Did you walk up there?'

Nick didn't answer, just stared back at Wilson.

'Was it the day you finally got your gold medal?'

Again Nick did not answer but looked genuinely surprised, then a smile started to spread across his face.

'Maybe you didn't even see Stanley or the puppies but you definitely went up to the Crystal Palace Parade with Pamela on that Monday afternoon, didn't you?'

Nick gave a sort of chuckle and shrugged.

'Why would I want to go with her?'

'I don't know, Nick, but you were not at school that afternoon. You were a friend of Stanley's and you were the one who told Pamela about the puppies. If you can't tell me where you were or what you were doing on that day I can only come to the conclusion that you were with Pamela.'

Nick looked at each of them in turn. His mother was biting her nails and didn't take her eyes off him. He returned his gaze to Wilson.

'Can you prove it?'

'When the forensic team went through Pamela's bag, her pink rucksack, they found a diary. She mentions the puppies and the old man and her 'friend' who we deduce is you. Also you were seen outside the school with Pamela by two separate people at lunchtime on that day. They have recently come forward to give us that information.'

Nick frowned, shook his head and took a deep breath.

'She was upset about the puppies. I tried to comfort her but she wouldn't listen.'

He smiled, then crossed his arms as if hugging himself and started to chuckle quietly.

'It was so easy. She was so nice. It was so easy.'

Nick sat there with his shoulders shaking, a strange sound that appeared to be laughter rippling around the room, then there was silence.

Valerie Jones sat frozen, unable to move. Wilson was momentarily lost for words. Mrs Powell, who had covered her mouth with her hands, spoke through her fingers and broke the silence.

'Oh, Nick, what have you done? What have you done this time?'

SALLY

The staffroom was packed. Sally squeezed on to the end of a chair with Carol and put her mug of tea on the floor.

'What's all this about, do you know?'

Carol took her glasses off and rubbed the lenses with her jumper. She spoke without looking up. 'It must be the girl who was murdered.'

'Oh, do you think they know who did it?'

'Maybe. There's that policeman who's been hanging around the school, over by the coffee machine with Miss Lloyd and Valerie Jones.'

At the end of morning lessons an announcement had come over the tannoy:

'Would all teachers attend an urgent meeting in the main staffroom at 1pm this lunchtime.'

The tannoy was rarely used. In Sally's short time at the school she had only heard it once and that was for a fire drill. Lessons were started and finished by a shrill bell. There was an air of expectancy, people were chatting in small groups but not really concentrating, everyone had their eye on the door or glanced over in the direction of the coffee machine. Who had called this meeting?

A few minutes later the headmaster swept in, accompanied by his secretary, and wearing his academic gown, something he usually only did for formal occasions such as prize-giving or parents' evenings. At his entrance, a natural hush fell over the room and all heads turned to face him as he took up a position halfway down the room, under the clock and facing the windows. Miss Lloyd, Valerie Jones and Detective Inspector Wilson walked across to stand next to him.

'Thank you for coming everyone. I have called this meeting because I have some important information that I want to share with you. It concerns Pamela Webb, the first-year pupil who has been missing for the past three months and whose body was found last week. We now have some new information concerning the case and I would like to hand you over to Detective Inspector Wilson.'

The headmaster stood to one side and Wilson moved into the space. Miss Lloyd was behind him with her arms folded. She stood erect with her neck stretching forward, chin up, looking beyond them all through the windows to the wintery trees outside. Valerie Jones was biting her lip but also stood with her arms folded looking down at the floor. It was clear that both of the women knew what Detective Inspector Wilson was about to say.

'As you know, the body of Pamela Webb was found last week in the tunnel under the road at Crystal Palace. The cause of death has been established as strangulation. We have also arrested a child from this school, a boy in the fourth year, and will be charging him with manslaughter on the grounds of diminished responsibility. His name is Nicholas Powell.'

There was a communal intake of breath. Not all the staff knew who Nick was, but the severity of the crime sent a chill through them all. Wilson cleared his throat and continued.

'At this stage, we would ask you all not to speak to the press. If you are approached by anyone please refer them to the official channels through the school. The story will be in the national newspapers tomorrow and also on the television news. This has been a high-profile case and public interest has been strong. Obviously our thoughts are with Pamela's family at this difficult time. I would like to take this opportunity of thanking all the staff here for their cooperation in helping solve this case. I'm just sorry it has had such a tragic outcome.'

Miss Lloyd stepped forward.

'Thank you, Detective Inspector, and on behalf of the staff I would like to say how we have appreciated your work here and the unobtrusive and efficient way you have gone about your business. It has been a deeply unsettling time for us all and a difficult term for teachers and pupils alike.

'On that note I would like to say that if any of the pupils appear upset or in any way affected by the news that will break tomorrow, please refer them in the first instance to their senior tutor or to any of us senior staff. Or indeed, if you feel able, then talk to them yourselves. It may be that they just need some reassurance or comforting.'

Miss Lloyd's voice wavered slightly on the word 'comforting' and she turned to the headmaster to conclude the proceedings.

He did so in a perfunctory manner, echoing the thanks of both Wilson and Miss Lloyd, but as usual the staff only half listened. He was not a good speaker, seeming to lack conviction in whatever he said and his tone did not distinguish between important or mundane facts, so everything was delivered in a dull drone. Once the senior staff and policeman had left the room, people started speaking quietly to each other.

'What on earth could the "diminished responsibility" be?'

'Wasn't he involved in something last year?'

'Always seemed such a pleasant lad.'

'It just goes to show.'

Sally sat and stared out of the window, thinking of all the times she had had Nick in her class. Apart from being late he had never done anything out of the ordinary. She had not seen him bully any of the other boys or act aggressively. He had never appeared to lose his temper or even argue with anyone. He had been pretty well-behaved apart from the absences and a few missed homeworks. She had not seen him drawing lurid violent acts on the back of his paper as some boys did, nor had she seen him scratching into the table legs with a lino cutter or crushing pieces of charcoal underfoot. No, he had seemed so ordinary. It was now this very ordinariness that disturbed her. She felt deceived.

'Did you teach him?'

Andy stood with his back to the window, then sat down next to her.

'Yes.'

She wasn't sure if she was ready to speak. She was still shocked by the news that a pupil in her class had killed someone.

'I taught him last year. He wasn't there for most of it of course, once he was sent away.'

Sally turned to look at him; her mouth felt dry.

'Yes, what happened? Why was he sent away?'

'He strung up some kid in a disused factory and left him hanging there. Fortunately, some other kids cut him down or....'

It was left unsaid and nasty images swarmed into her head.

'So was he sent to borstal?'

'Yes, something like that. He was away for six months.'

'Why weren't we told?'

'Most of the staff already knew about it but with new teachers, well, maybe they thought he should have a fresh start.'

Sally started to feel angry.

'Yes, but we should have been told. I have had a kid in my class who did something like that, something pretty serious and yet no one told me. All of Nick's teachers should have been informed. We should have been told. He was dangerous.'

Andy put his hand on Sally's arm then withdrew it.

'Yes, you're right.'

Sally sat back in her chair and folded her arms. She was still angry.

'So, if most people here, apart from me, knew about Nick's previous conviction, why wasn't he questioned more thoroughly? Surely he must have been a strong suspect?'

'You would have thought so.'

There was a silence, which Andy broke by asking if he could get her a cup of tea.

'No, I think I need to get some fresh air.'

As Sally walked towards the door, Mr Gibson stood talking to Valerie Jones. His face was pale and strained at the recent news and he appeared to be deep in conversation. Sally's approach seemed to give him an excuse for a break in his discussion with Valerie. He moved to the door and held it open, waving her through with a slight flourish.

Sally passed through but couldn't even bring herself to look at him.

VALERIE

Strictly speaking, there was no need to meet at the pub any more. Now it was established that Nick had killed Pamela, and he had been handed over to the psychiatric branch to confirm his mental condition, the case was more or less over. However, Valerie had not seen Wilson since the day they questioned Nick, and she had a few questions herself. Also, Friday evenings with Ray in the pub had become the thing that Valerie Jones most looked forward to all week.

She kicked her shoes off under the table and smiled as Wilson mimed with a series of gestures whether or not she wanted peanuts. She nodded and felt totally relaxed. As she looked across to the bar where Ray was chatting to the landlord, Valerie had to admit that her feelings were becoming more complicated. Did she fancy him? She thought she might do but didn't totally understand why. She considered Ray still standing at the bar. He was tallish, about six foot, with a definite middle-age spread that demonstrated his love of food and beer. Normally this would have put her off, but not in this case. His hair was receding and she had noticed flakes of dry skin on his neck. She didn't understand why she felt herself attracted to Ray Wilson, a balding slightly overweight policeman. Her own husband was younger and marginally better looking, but that didn't seem to be the point.

Ray set the drinks carefully on the table and pulled a packet of peanuts from his pocket. Valerie leaned forward and sipped her lager and lime.

'Now Detective Inspector, I have a number of questions.'

'Fire away.'

He kept his eyes on her as he downed half the glass in one gulp.

Valerie sat back and looked directly at him.

'Firstly, what was in Pamela's diary that incriminated Nick?'

'Well, not much actually. She mentioned the puppies and how much she wanted one. She was worried that they would be killed by the grumpy old man so she was willing to bunk off school in order to save them. She said she was going with a friend but didn't actually name him.'

'So what made you so sure it was Nick?'

'He was seen with Pamela by two people that lunchtime.'

Valerie frowned.

'Why didn't they come forward before now?'

'The first person was the cleaner, Iris. Do you know her? Yes, a fair-haired woman, part-time, she also cleans one of the houses opposite the school. Well, she came to see me last week. She was agitated and nervous, said she had wanted to speak to me earlier but was afraid she might get the sack.'

'Blimey what had she done?'

'It seems she had been having a fling with Arthur Simmons and the day Pamela disappeared they had an assignation, my word not hers, in the small cupboard by the front office. Iris had her back to the wall and could see out of the small window to the school gate. She saw Pamela waiting and the next time she looked, she saw her walking away.'

'With Nick?'

'Yes, with Nick.'

'The poor woman was so frightened she would be sacked she kept her mouth shut hoping Pamela might still turn up. When the body was found she felt she had to come forward. The silly thing is she could have just told me or anyone that she was putting brooms away and happened to look out of the window. No one would have been any the wiser. It seems she couldn't see past her guilt.'

'And the second person?'

'A sixth-form pupil, an American boy who started late and his first day at school was the Monday Pamela disappeared. He arrived at lunchtime with his father and noticed Pamela waiting by the bike racks.'

'Why didn't he come forward earlier?'

'Didn't think he needed to. He had seen Pamela and that was all as far as he was concerned. A couple of teachers told him to come and talk to me and when he did I showed him a few photos, including one of Nick. He picked him out as having been with Pamela walking away from the bike racks. No one had actually seen Nick and Pamela together at Crystal Palace but that didn't matter once Nick confessed.'

'And the fire at the gypsy's caravan, was that anything to do with Nick?'

'No, I don't think so. It was a piece of luck for Nick though as it almost gave him someone to blame for Pamela's murder, complete with all evidence destroyed.'

Valerie finished her drink and shivered as the door opened and a new group of people came in, bringing a wave of cold air. She looked directly at Wilson.

'There's something I can't get out of my head. I keep hearing it and it gives me the creeps. It's the sound of Nick's laughter.'

SALLY

The staffroom was transformed. Most of the chairs had been cleared away to make space for dancing. A few coffee tables and chairs had been shifted to the tea area that had now become the bar. Mr Gibson stood behind it polishing glasses as he took them out of cardboard boxes. The disco was in the corner and already the lights in front of the deck were flashing green and red. Heavy curtains not usually pulled now shut out the dark trees and the street lights, giving an impression of intimacy.

Miss Lloyd was standing at the bar holding a glass of Sherry. She wore a black dress with a sparkly brooch and was laughing at something Mr Gibson said. She hadn't been sure about coming this evening as disco music wasn't something she enjoyed, but the opportunity to dress up and socialise had lured her out. As she had powdered her nose, sitting comfortably at her dressing table, she told herself she could always leave early. Snapping shut the jewellery box she reassured herself that other older members of staff would also be there. Making small talk with other men's wives was something she had got used to a long time ago.

'Excuse me, Miss Lloyd.'

Arthur Simmons thumped a large crate of beer onto the counter next to her. For a moment she hardly recognised him in a large collared shirt and fatly knotted tie. 'This should keep the blokes happy.'

'Yes, indeed.'

Strange how different he looked out of his overalls. She was touched by the effort he had made with his appearance. So many of the younger male teachers were wearing jeans and open-necked shirts, but Arthur actually looked very smart. Miss Lloyd spotted Mr Booth and his wife who seemed genuinely pleased to see her. Mr Booth sat the two women at one of the tables then went to get them all a drink. Miss Lloyd forgot to feel grateful for this small act of inclusion and started to enjoy herself.

'One two, one two.'

Mark, the biology teacher, tested the microphone.

Miss Lloyd turned to Mrs Booth.

'I say, that's awfully loud,' and the two women giggled together.

The room was filling up.

Sally stood sipping a beer with Carol the pottery teacher. They had met in the pub beforehand and come with a couple of Carol's male friends. Sally knew them vaguely and remembered that Ian was a good dancer. Unlike many men, he didn't need a vat of alcohol to get him on the dance floor.

'One two, one two. Good evening everybody and welcome to the Christmas disco. Here's a track to get you in the festive mood.'

No one danced to 'Rudolph the Red-Nosed Reindeer' but knocked back drinks in readiness for a good dance track.

It came in the form of James Brown and suddenly the dance floor was dotted with younger teachers. Miss Lloyd balked at both the volume and the explicit lyrics but was determined not to be defeated by either. She raised her glass at Mrs Booth, downed another Sherry and tapped her foot experimentally.

Arthur Simmons was enjoying himself in the role of barman. He had convinced his wife not to come, by explaining he was going to work and would just be shifting chairs and clearing up. She wouldn't really know anyone and so had been persuaded to go to the pub with a couple of girlfriends.

He watched with interest two young teachers in their short dresses and black tights. Arthur didn't really like all this dancing on your own and had been a bit of a Teddy Boy in his day. He was over the moon when a Chuck Berry track came on. It may have been the beer and the whisky from his hip flask that gave him a reckless courage. He grabbed Miss Sargent the French teacher by the hand, pulled her onto the dance floor and they started to jive.

'Oh, look at Arthur Simmons.' Miss Lloyd was clapping in time to the music. Mark the DJ knew he was onto a good thing and followed with 'Blue Suede Shoes'.

Mr Booth pulled Miss Lloyd to her feet, despite her faint protests that she had never 'jitterbugged' in her life. She was nimble and though neither she nor Mr Booth knew the steps, they muddled through and enjoyed themselves.

But Arthur Simmons and Miss Sargent were the stars of the floor. He spun her round and pulled her to him then released her, a slight push on her waist and she turned on a sixpence. Underarm then over, nimble and agile they moved as one. As the track finished, everyone clapped and Arthur Simmons kissed Miss Sargent's hand as they left the floor. The music changed. Carol appeared at Sally's side and dug her in the ribs.

'I've got to talk to you, Sal.'

'What's it about?

They escaped to the quiet of the ladies' cloakroom.

Carol checked all the cubicles were empty, then launched into a long description of a conversation she had just had with an English teacher called Barbara.

'It seems she and Andy have been going out for over a year, since last summer, before you and I started here. You could have knocked me down with a feather. I mean, he seemed so keen on you.'

Sally sighed. 'Typical.'

Carol continued, and there seemed to be no stopping her. 'What on earth does he see in her? She's so dreamy and floaty like she wants to be a poet. Not a patch on you, Sal.'

Sally grunted and felt alternately angry and disappointed. She had started to consider Andy a definite possibility in the boyfriend stakes, had thought about him quite a lot outside school and looked forward to their conversations in the staffroom. Had she imagined his interest? No, he always made a point of sitting next to her at break, asked if she had seen certain exhibitions, wanted her opinion on different painters. Surely he had hinted she should visit him in Scotland and was horrified she had never even set foot in the country. All of that had been real and he did genuinely seem to like her, but obviously not enough.

Sally returned to the disco and went across to the bar where Valerie Jones and the Detective Inspector were queuing for drinks. Carol came up and nudged her.

'Look.'

Andy and Barbara were dancing a smoochy number and holding each other very close. As they turned slowly around the floor Andy caught Sally's eye and registered her expression. She turned her back and ordered a beer for herself and red wine for Carol. Putting her purse away, she turned to find Andy at the bar holding two empty glasses.

'I wanted to tell you.'

'But you didn't.'

'I'm sorry.'

Sally shrugged and turned away, not wanting to talk any more. She carried the drinks across to Carol and set them on a table. She would have to speak to the DJ. He was playing far too many slow numbers.

Valerie Jones was feeling quite drunk and vaguely reckless as she stood with Ray at the bar. Miss Lloyd had invited him to the Christmas disco as a way of thanking him for his work in solving the case of Pamela Webb. He hadn't been keen to come but felt it would have been churlish to refuse the invitation. He was not a fan of discos and didn't really know anyone apart from Valerie. He insisted on buying her a drink as soon as he arrived. Valerie's cheeks were very pink and she was starting to feel slightly bold.

'I will miss our Friday meetings, Ray.'

'Yes, but the case is now thankfully closed.'

That was unfair Valerie thought. He knows I am not talking just about the case but about our friendship. She tried again.

'Might you call in sometimes for a drink at that pub, after work, on a Friday?'

'Maybe. It depends where I am. Nothing is certain in my job.'

He drained his glass, leaving a ring of foam at the bottom.

'Come on.'

Wilson turned and steered her onto the dance floor.

SALLY

The table in the kitchen was covered by a white damask cloth, and Sally noticed the words 'Savoy Hotel' woven into the border. An elegant bent candelabra with three stumps of red candles stood next to a miniature Christmas tree in the centre of the table. The knives were all different versions of the same design, bone handles discoloured like old fingernails and with Sheffield steel blades. Several of the forks were bent and tarnished and the spoons ranged from large dessert down to teaspoon. The overall effect was a sort of antique jumble sale.

'Sherry for the cooks.'

Reg came into the kitchen carrying a bottle and a half-filled glass that slopped precariously. He poured a full glass for Sally and Claire who were turning the roast potatoes.

They had decided to have a Christmas dinner in the house before all leaving for their parents' homes in a variety of distant towns, villages or suburbs. The kitchen gave the occasion a richness and style as the December afternoon darkened to evening and candles lit the table. Once the food was ready they switched out all the electric lights. A row of fat candles stood spluttering on the mantelpiece above the boiler, and several were clustered on the deep windowsills facing up to the front garden and the heath. An old-fashioned lantern stood by the sink, its flame wavering in the strong draught from the nearby door. This soft lighting suited the kitchen, and was a reminder of the way things used to be done. The dumbwaiter stood static in one corner and the dim outline of the piano was visible in another. In the shadows, the objects blurred and became timeless.

Ten people sat down to eat, and after the plates were cleared someone suggested singing carols. They didn't get all the words right and not everyone sang in tune. Reg hummed along, his eyes half-closed as if he were both shutting out and letting in the past and the present. They ran out of carols to sing. Someone made coffee and Reg took out a box of chocolate liqueurs, the silver papers catching the light and glistening among the pudding plates and pulled crackers. People started clearing away. This, after all, wasn't proper Christmas, just a precursor to the one they would spend with their families. In some ways, though, it was a slice of something richer. There were connections, as thin as the chocolate papers, with the two hundred Christmases that had taken place in that kitchen before. Dregs of sugary Sherry stuck to the glasses. It was time to wash up, pack their bags and go home.

Sally waited by the front door with her belongings gathered around her feet. The hastily wrapped presents and assorted clothes spilled out of the tops of baskets and carrier bags. She had not packed carefully or economically, knowing there was plenty of space in her father's van. Her first term's teaching was over but already it felt as though she had been at the school far longer. She still felt too young and was unsure if she would continue once the probationary year was completed. The job had flooded her life in a way she had not anticipated, with weekends spent preparing for the following week, trying out samples to check if a technique worked, finding interesting objects to draw in the woods or rummaging in skips and researching artists in the library. She would walk across the heath with lesson ideas tumbling through her head, then on the actual day it would all turn out differently. She had done no painting since September and hardly any drawing, and wondered if she would ever be able to fit it in again.

She had not spoken to Andy since the Christmas disco, and missed their conversations and the sense of anticipation before break or lunch in case he might be in the staffroom. His presence had been one of the things she most looked forward to at the school. In her imagination, she had climbed the crumbling steps of the old Crystal Palace Gardens with him and taken photos standing near prehistoric monsters on the lake. All of that would need to be erased from her mind. So, too, her imaginary walks with him along a wild coast of Scotland wearing a tartan scarf. This was starting to feel like an image stuck on a tin of shortbread rather than an actual possibility. Once again she thought of Freddy, and remembered she still hadn't found out what had happened to him.

Most of all, Sally was still angry about the whole situation of Nick. She kept going through questions in her mind. Why had she not been told about his previous conviction? Had it been dangerous to have him in her class? What was meant by 'diminished responsibility'? What would happen to Nick? There seemed to be such a lack of communication. A knock on the door broke into her thoughts; it was her father.

'Are you ready then?'

They carried the boxes and bags through the doorway past Reg's room where the packet of bacon and clean laundry waited on the chest as usual.

ALAN

They had arranged to meet at Greenwich Station. Marie walked down from Deptford, and as she crossed the bridge over the creek saw a horse and cart and heard a faint cry of 'rag and bone' as it turned into the scrapyard. The small crane that hung over the water's edge and the gas cylinder with the scratched red lettering from the 1930s had become familiar landmarks on her way to Alan's shop. It was Christmas Eve, dull and grey, and the weather didn't feel particularly festive. As she approached Greenwich she saw the Christmas tree tied to the top of the mast of the Cutty Sark and the lamps of the stalls as she passed the market passage.

Marie was a little nervous at the prospect of spending Christmas with Alan's mother and Peggy down in Reigate. It seemed he had asked her on impulse when they sat in his kitchen following the police incident. He had apologised for his behaviour at the party and tried to explain why he felt old and boring among all Marie's art school crowd. She was slightly incredulous and explained how fed up she was with so many young men in tight trousers, how she found their drinking and drug taking frankly boring. She liked Alan because he had strong interests, yes even old railways, and she felt she could trust him. This was important to her. It was then that he asked her to come to Reigate for Christmas. It seemed he hadn't quite known he was going to ask her, but once he had blurted it out he was glad, and even more relieved when she had said yes. It had been the same as his first ever invitation to have a drink, completely unplanned and unexpected but successful.

Marie had never been to Reigate and had not yet met Alan's mother. She had found two prints of Reigate in the 1820s and had tinted and framed them as a present. Pleased with the result, she hoped Alan's mother would like them. Her bags were quite heavy and Alan was already waiting at the station with a small duffle bag.

'Well, you travel light. Is Santa taking your presents for you?'

The train took them to Waterloo where they changed for Reigate. Marie sat opposite Alan. She had taken off her thick woolly beret and was ruffling her hair.

'Now tell me again, Alan. What happened when the police turned up?'

'How many times do you want to hear this story?'

'Lots. Go on.'

'Well, as I've already told you, I got out of that tunnel as fast as I could, but a woman in one of the prefabs had seen me go in and already phoned the police. So as I climbed out of the manhole cover, two officers were waiting. I think they were surprised I was so pleased to see them – it saved me phoning 999 from the phone box on the parade. Obviously they were suspicious of me, and when I told them what I had seen in the tunnel under the road they wanted to take me in for questioning.'

'Will you tell your mother you were arrested?'

'I will tell her exactly the same as I told you.'

Marie looked out at the passing fields and her expression became more serious.

'It must have been awful though, seeing that poor kid.'

'Yes, it was a sort of horrible slow dawning, because it just looked like a pile of rags at first, but then there was that smell.'

Marie shuddered.

'The camera helped. I was able to keep my distance and just look through the lens. The close-up of her face

284

is not something I will forget in a hurry. Once I was certain, and had photos as proof, I just wanted to get out of there.'

'I was worried when Rob came to take me to the police station. I couldn't believe you were a suspect.'

'Well, look at it from their point of view. You see a grown man climbing out of a manhole cover and then this man tells you that the body of a girl is lying down there under the road. The description of the girl matches that of the one who had been missing since September. There's been huge publicity about the case.'

'Will you be in the papers?'

'Yes, but no picture, only my name.'

'So you will be famous for your railway discoveries, but not in quite the way you planned.'

'So it seems.'

Marie stood up and pulled a magazine from one of her bags.

'There's a strange little link with the Pissarro paintings and the murdered girl. I read about it in that magazine Rob got for you, the article that explains all the locations of the London paintings. Yes, here it is.'

She flicked open the page.

'This painting, "A view from Sydenham Hill". Look, there is a house in the distance, in the centre, across the fields in an almost rural setting. Underneath is a photo of the same view now, completely filled in with buildings, but that house is still there, totally recognisable despite the larger trees and the blue Cortina parked outside.'

'What is the link with the murdered girl?'

'Well, the house is opposite the school she went to, where she was last seen alive.'

PAMELA

I waited a few minutes and then he came. He said we had to walk. It turned out to be a long way and it was uphill. I started to worry about missing lessons. After a long time we got to the top of the hill and walked along to where the buses wait. I'd never noticed before but there is a sunken bit of ground near to the roundabout and that's where the old man's caravan is. The whole area looks a bit of a dump. There is just an Alsatian, a big barking dog tied up outside the caravan. I can't see any puppies. He goes inside to speak to the old man and there are no puppies in there either. I feel bad. I have never bunked off school before. Is it all for nothing? Has he killed the puppies? How did he kill them?

I'm upset. I want a cuddly little puppy to look after. I've been looking forward to it so much. I can't help crying and it's difficult to stop. He puts his hand on my shoulder and says he's sorry the puppies are gone. Still I can't stop crying.

He walks away a few steps and says he wants to show me something. It is a special place, a secret and hidden place that no one knows about.

I'm still shaking a bit and crying, but also interested. We have to climb back up the steps but just before the top there is an opening with a cover that he lifts off. He says we have to go down there and shows me the ladder. I'm not sure. I am still upset and have run out of tissues. Part of me wants to go home and lie on my bed with Billy, my toy dog, but the other part of me likes exploring secret places. It is a bit of a squeeze with my rucksack. He says I should take it off but I won't. At the bottom of the ladder is a tunnel. I have to bend a bit to walk and I follow his torch. I'm not scared by the darkness. After a few minutes we come out into a large space. There is light coming in from a strip above and we both blink to get our eyes used to it. It is a special place like an underground church. Why is it here? He says you get the best view of the roof by lying down, so we sit on a pile of coal with rags on top. He shines the torch up and we can see the patterns of the arches coming together like trees over our heads. I sit up and feel tearful again thinking of the puppies. Nick puts his arm around me and tells me not to be upset any more. He turns my head towards him. I think he's going to kiss me.